BOOK 4 OF MORNA'S LEGACY

LOVE BEYOND MEASURE

A SCOTTISH TIME TRAVELING ROMANCE

BETHANY CLAIRE

For Papa

Chapter 1

"Pssst…"

Believing he'd heard something, but not sure enough to fully turn his head toward the sound, the corner of Cooper's right brow lifted slightly.

I grinned, making sure not to stick my head out too far past the archway. I didn't want anyone sitting in the outdoor aisles to see me. "Pssst…" I said it once more, waiting for the child to turn his head in my direction so that I could wave him toward me.

His bow tie hung crooked and his dirty blonde hair, which I'd gelled down only hours before, now stuck up in every direction, unruly curls descending over his face. He turned his head slowly, deep green eyes widening at the sight of me before the fading sun hit him square on the nose, spreading a soft light across the dash of freckles across his face. He squinted trying to make me out properly while his little legs fidgeted as he restrained from stepping away from his assigned spot.

Cooper's mouth opened and then closed as I silently waved a finger in front of my lips, pleading with him to stay quiet. Turning the inside of my finger toward me, I extended it out so that I could gesture for him to join me.

It took only a brief moment before his feet found their freedom, and he ran toward me so quickly that I hardly had time to open my arms to him before he sailed into me. I smiled into his collar as he spoke, in what I could only assume was his full-hearted effort at a whisper, although it truly ended up sounding more like a breathy squeal.

"I thought maybe you were Dad! He bet me five dollars I couldn't stand still until the end of the ceremony, and I been just waitin' for him to try to make me lose."

"That does sound just like him, doesn't it? He's actually waiting for us in the car. How about the three of us get out of here?" I swung him onto my hip, not the least bit worried about smushing any of the lacy mess that covered me head to toe.

"What?" He made no effort to whisper this time.

I quickly took off in the direction of the car before we were noticed. It wouldn't do for anyone to see that the bride and groom, along with their son, were about to bail away from their own wedding. I wanted to be at least off of the estate property before word got out.

"Shh…" I said nothing else, moving toward our favorite spot by the water. Thankfully, it also happened to be far enough away from the wedding crowd that no one would hear or find us there.

"Are we going to the swing?" He managed a real whisper that time, and the sweetness of it made me lean in to kiss him hard on his cheek. Still young enough not to have total disdain for his mother's affections, he smiled and lay his head against my shoulder.

"Yes, we are. I want to talk to you a minute. Just you and me, before we go join your dad. How'd you know I was taking you to the swing?"

"Oh Mom, don't you member that we always go there when we need *you and me* time at Grandfather's?"

"Of course, I remember. We've just really never discussed it, so I'm surprised you picked up on it is all."

"Yep. I did."

"I can see that. You're very smart for a four year old." And he was—exceedingly so. If it wasn't for his small size, most would guess him to be a good two years older.

"Yep, but I'm really four and seven months. That's

almost five."

"Oh my, and you're quite sure of yourself, too. That trait comes from your father."

By now, we'd reached what, in my opinion, was the most beautiful part of my parents' grand estate on Lake Placid. Nestled under a wide, broad-leafed tree that stood out among the many pine and spruce trees scattered throughout, hung a large white swing built so that it hung perfectly from one of the tree's largest branches. Large cushions enveloped the floating chair. I collapsed into it, still holding on to Cooper as we fell back into the softness together.

"Yep."

I tugged playfully on one of his loose curls so that he'd look at me. "Alright. Enough with the 'yeps.'" He giggled sheepishly at his orneriness. "I want to talk to you about something serious for a minute."

He scooted away from my arm so that he could regard me fully and, with all the determination he could muster, pulled the expression on his face into one of sheer seriousness. "I'm ready."

He regarded me sternly so that I would get on with whatever it was I wished to discuss with him.

"Ok. What did you think about all of this today?"

His eyebrows scrunched together as if he were thinking very hard about how he should answer. I reached out to squeeze his hand, reassuring him that he could say whatever he wished. "I...I think it's weird."

"How do you mean, Coop? What was weird about it?"

"Well, I know that I'm only little, but I been thinkin' about this real hard."

I smiled, no doubt he had done just that. "I'm sure you have."

He glanced up at me beneath thick brown lashes, twirling his little fingers in nervous swirls before continuing. "And...I know that Grandfather thinks that moms and dads should be married, but I like things the way they are now. I heard something…"

He hesitated, gauging my reaction. He had a penchant for eavesdropping, and I could tell he worried I'd get on to him for doing it again. "It's alright. What did you hear?'

"Last night, I heard Grams talking to Aunt Jane and Aunt Lily, and I didn't hear everything, but she said it was wrong of Grandfather to push you into this, Mom. That you and Dad liked each other too much to get married."

It sounded just like my mother. I only wished she'd said it to me and not my sisters. Perhaps I would've decided to call this thing off before the day of the actual wedding. "And what do you think about that?"

Cooper shrugged a little as he spoke, "I think she's right, Mama. All Grams and Grandfather do is fight, and they're married. So do Aunt Lily and Uncle Jim. I don't want you and Pops to start fighting."

"Pops?" I laughed at the oddity of it. He'd never called Jeffrey 'Pops' once in his life.

"I heard Dad calling Bebop that and I liked it. Thought I would try it out."

"I see." I grinned, messing with his hair. "Well, I agree with you and so does 'Pops.' Your father and I can't get married. It wouldn't be fair of us to do that to this family. But that's why I wanted to talk to you, we *are* still a family. No matter whether me and your Dad are married, the three of us are a family. Do you understand that?"

"Yes, Mom." He sighed, clearly believing that I had no reason to doubt his understanding much of anything. Honestly, I really didn't.

"And one more thing before we join your father. I don't want you to think that because you're little that I think less of what you think. If anything, I value what you think more than anyone else because you are little."

That...and I was slightly afraid he was already smarter

than me, but I certainly wasn't going to say something like that to my son. I very much wanted him to think I was the smartest person on earth for at least another decade.

"Ok, Mom. Can we go find Dad now?"

"Absolutely. Let's get out of here." Lifting Cooper out of the swing, I wrestled with the globs of white lace that gathered around me until I once again stood on two feet. Grabbing his hand, I peeked around the tree to make sure the coast was clear and we took off, running toward the front of the house where his father waited with our escape vehicle.

"Are we going back to the City?" Cooper's words came out choppy, bouncing with every step his short stride took.

"For a minute we are, but I'll do you one better. What's the one place you've always wanted to go?"

In that instant, his little feet stopped moving completely, and I nearly took a tumble with the jolt at the sudden stop of his movement.

"No! A plane? Oh Mama, am I *finally* gonna get to go on a plane?"

I laughed. He was four, nearly five truthfully, but still, how long could he really have been waiting? "Yes, you are. You're going to go on a job with me."

We neared the vehicle. Jeffrey must've seen us for he started the car, awaiting our approach.

"Where are we goin'?"

"Scotland."

"Why?"

"I'll tell you in the car."

* * *

"Do you mind taking off your jacket so that I can drape it over Coop? He's asleep. Can you hear him snoring?"

"Gladly. Sweet sound, isn't it?" Jeffrey held his arm out to me so that I would pull on his sleeve while he shrugged out of the tux jacket. Once free of it, I twisted so that I could reach into the backseat and drape it over our sleeping son.

"The sweetest."

Once I faced the front of the car again, Jeffrey reached over to squeeze my shoulder. "We're getting close. Do you want to call the office to see if he's even there? It's pretty late."

I shook my head, confident that nothing much had changed in Mr. Perdie's routine since I took off work three days before for my wedding. "No, he'll be there. He works so much he wouldn't even come to our wedding, not that there was a wedding to come to, but you know what I mean."

"Alright. Are you going to wear that?" He glanced at me, keeping one eye on the road.

"What are you saying? Do you think it's too much?" I laughed, but quickly silenced myself so that I wouldn't wake Cooper. "Don't worry. He'll be the only one in the office at this hour, and he'll be so buried up to his elbows in work of some kind that I doubt he'll even take notice of the fact that I'm in a wedding gown. So yes, I am going to wear this. I need to talk to him before we do anything else to make sure it's alright that I start the job early."

For the first time since all of the wedding madness began a few days earlier, I thought about the new job. Mr. Perdie had come into my office literally an hour before I was due to take off for the next two weeks for my wedding.

Apparently, an anonymous Scottish land owner had called Perdie, willing to donate a large sum of money to the magazine under the condition that we would do a lengthy piece on Scotland in an upcoming issue.

The call must have come as quite a shock to my boss. Not only did our readership seem to decline daily but, unbeknownst to the anonymous donor (or perhaps he knew quite well), our small travel magazine neared the brink of death, with only five more issues guaranteed. His donation would ensure that we could all keep our jobs for at least another five years.

Even more stunning, and the fact that had caused me to spill my sacred cup of coffee, was that the donor requested that I do the article. All of it. Writing. Photography. He specifically wanted me to author the piece.

I worked hard, but being one of the newest photographers at the magazine, I'd never been given a piece of significant value. I was usually assigned articles like, *How To Pack Everything You Need For 10 days In A Carry-On,* and, *Best Airport Restaurants.* As of yet, the only photography I'd been assigned by the magazine had been photos of the inside of a suitcase and airport. Why the man would request that I do the article was beyond me.

After I'd overcome my initial shock, Perdie and I scheduled my trip for right after my honeymoon, but seeing as that would no longer happen, I saw no reason to wait another second. I imagined that Mr. Perdie would feel the same, especially since the receival of the donor's money was contingent upon my flight information being sent to him directly after its booking.

"Hey...where'd you go?" Jeffrey pulled into the parking garage below my office building and grasped my hand lightly to pull me from my reflective trance. "We're here."

"Sorry, I was just thinking about all of this. Crazy, isn't it?"

The corner of Jeffrey's brow pulled up quizzically, much like Cooper's had done earlier. They were so much alike in behavior and outward appearance that even I often had a hard time believing that they weren't actually biologically related.

"Which part, Grace? The 'you and me' bit, or this work stuff?"

I shrugged a bit, unbuckling and facing him as he slid into a parking spot and stilled the car. "All of it. Everything that seems to be going on." I reached out to grab both his hands. "I'm so sorry, Jeffrey. I can't express to you," I suddenly found myself quite choked up. "What it means...what it means that you've allowed me to pull you into all of this. And I don't just mean now. Always. Our whole lives it seems like I've been dragging you into one mess or another."

He frowned, pulling his hands free so that he could cup both sides of my face. "You dragged me into nothing, Grace. Ever. Your father did, when it came to law school and then joining his practice, but you never did. You're my best friend, and I consider you my closest family. There is nothing in this world that I wouldn't do for you."

"Clearly." I smiled into his palms thinking of the attire we were both wearing now. No matter how platonic our love for one another, he'd been willing to marry me at my father's request. "I love you, too. And gosh—Coop and I, we just couldn't do without you. Are you sure you're fine with me taking him along on the trip?"

Jeffrey released my face and glanced lovingly into the backseat of the car. "Absolutely. I'd come too, but I have one last case I have to finish before I rid myself of your father's firm. Coop will love every minute of it and, since we're going to delay his entry into kindergarten for a year, I have no problem with it."

"Good. Well, I guess I better go talk to him. Shouldn't take me long. Be back shortly."

It took me a good minute and a half to swing my feet out of the vehicle and gather the train and fabric that surrounded my legs and ankles. I moved rather self-consciously through the parking garage, although I went unseen. While I had no qualms about Mr. Perdie seeing me in my wedding regalia, I didn't really want anyone else wondering who the nut was roaming around in a gown.

I found him in his office, as expected. His glasses set a bit crooked, a mustard stain on his tie. Looking at him, I worried a bit that he hadn't changed his clothes in the last three days. He was a kind enough man, but just glancing around his office caused a slight rise in my blood pressure. It was surely no wonder that the magazine struggled with organizational skills such as his. How many things that needed to be attended to fell through the cracks in the black hole that seemed to be Perdie's office?

"Mr. Perdie?"

He jerked up from his desk so quickly, his chair flipped backward onto the floor. "Grace! What in the bletherin' hell are you doing here? I mean, is everything alright? Of course, it mustn't be. You're still in your wedding dress."

He moved toward me quickly. I instinctively reached out to grasp his hand in reassurance. "Oh yes, everything's fine. We just called it off is all. Just drove in from ..."

The shrillness of the small man's voice interrupted me. "What do you mean, everything's fine? Didn't you just say you called it off? That's rarely a good thing."

I was utterly shocked to see such concern from him, and it made me believe that perhaps I'd judged him wrongly for many years. "Yes, I promise. Everything is great. We just, we couldn't go through with it. But, Jeffrey and Cooper are waiting in the car, so it was really no tragedy or anything."

He patted my hand in a grandfatherly manner, although still a good many years off from being old enough to be anyone's grandfather. "Well good, Grace. Honestly, I've never really seen it between the two of you. It shocked me when you announced you were to be married."

I squeezed his hand in return, a sudden sensation of closeness growing between me and my quirky boss that I'd never felt before. "Well, Mr. Perdie, I must say I'm rather surprised by you. I never knew you to be so perceptive."

"Ms. Mitchell, perhaps it is you who lacks perception. I can assure you it's not a new quality I have developed. I know most of the time it appears that I can hardly keep my head screwed on, but I do notice almost everything."

I smiled and nodded before continuing on with the reason

for my late night office visit. "I'd like to take on the Scotland job now if that's alright. Leave tomorrow if at all possible. And…" I hesitated. It didn't truly matter whether or not he objected, but I still hoped he would have no problems with Cooper coming along for the trip. "Cooper is coming with me. I hope that won't be a problem."

"Of course you may start right away. As long as you complete the article and do a wonderful job of it, I have no problem with you bringing along your son. I believe we will have more than enough from our benefactor to pay for his flight, as well. I will book the flight for you both right away and will forward you the details when complete. Pack your bags, dear."

I nodded. As he turned toward his desk, I started to take my leave, but not before I heard his voice, laced with anxiety, follow me down the corridor. "And for the love of all things holy, Grace. Do not screw this up. We'll be without our jobs by Christmas without this money."

Chapter 2

This time proved far easier than the last, but his scars still ached something dreadful. Each dab of the warm cloth that Morna pressed against the angry red line that now marked the entire length of his body caused him to grind his teeth to keep from screaming out.

"I'm sorry, lad, but I must first clean it before I place the salve upon it. Talk to me. It will help to distract ye from the pain a wee bit, though it must no be hurting ye as much as it did when ye first arrived here. Does it, Eoghanan?"

It took some effort to loosen his jaw enough to speak, but eventually he forced the words to come. "Nay, it doesna hurt as much as then, but if I were standing, it would do a fair job of bringing me to me knees, all the same." The old witch was right, releasing the tight clench of his jaw did seem to ease the pain a little, or at least it helped him to notice it less. Decidedly, he thought it best to keep talking. "I saw her again. The same lass as the last time. Her and the wee lad both."

"Ah, and what lass is this?"

Morna's voice gave nothing away, but her hand momentarily stilled along the side of his neck, all but confirming what he already suspected. She knew well enough the woman he spoke of.

"I suspect that ye know the lass far better than I, doona ye? I've only watched the lass, but ye have sent me to her twice."

This time the old woman remained entirely un-bothered, continuing her slow and steady cleansing of his injured side. "I doona wish to disappoint ye, but I am no familiar with who ye speak of, and I have sent ye nowhere, lad. 'Tis no the way this magic works."

Eoghanan struggled to sit up but was restrained by Morna's hand moving to press his shoulder back down onto the bed, causing his frustration to rise even further. "I doona believe ye. Is it no yer magic that no only brought me here but sends me back now? What I canna figure out is the purpose behind it. Why no send me back to a time earlier, but still in this verra spot if I canna yet go home? I doona know where I have been the last two times, but it wasna Scotland. I'd bet me verra life on that fact."

Eoghanan watched as resignation washed over his bed nurse. The lines of her face softened slightly. He hoped answers might finally come to him.

"Ach, ye are a stubborn lad, are ye no? But still...I suppose ye deserve an explanation, so that I shall try to give to ye." She pulled the cloth away from the top of Eoghanan's shoulder, her once red hair now graying from the effects of time, dipping into the water as she reached over the basin sitting beside her to ring it out before draping it over the side of the bowl. Hands free, she leaned back in her seat, crossing her arms before continuing. "Though, I'll no lay blame on meself for not providing ye one earlier. Ye were in such a rush to travel back to yer home, that ye wouldna have listened to anything that I said. Ye dinna even allow me the chance to tell ye that yer first travel wouldna be to the time ye wished it."

Eoghanan succeeded in sitting up this time, determined to look at Morna straight on as she spoke to him. His own red hair hung frustratingly in his face, covering his green eyes. He blew the strands upward to clear his vision before he spoke. "Aye, I am in a hurry to return home. Me brother's wife is with child, and I doona wish to miss the bairn's arrival. I have stayed too long here."

Morna's head shook forcefully in denial of what he'd said. "No. Ye havena stayed nearly long enough. Do ye no remember what happened to ye the first time I sent ye back? Why yer wound split partially open, and ye nearly died...again! If I were ye, I wouldna wish to go knocking on death's door another time. Ye probably havena heard it, but there's something that people say in this time—third time's a charm. Ye go visiting death again, and he might just decide to answer the door." She paused momentarily, lowering her voice which had grown rather excited. "That being said, I will do all that I can to make sure ye will be strong enough to return home before the child's arrival, but in order for ye to be so, we must keep working to send ye back, but no so far so quickly."

A fortnight earlier, after spending months nearly entirely bedridden, Morna's announcement that she was ready to use her magic on him had indeed excited him so much that he'd not allowed any further instruction or explanation. He demanded that she use it on him at once.

The result was an experience so shocking and strange that Eoghanan still could not fully process all that he'd seen, only holding on to the one piece of serenity he'd found in the chaotic world he'd been sent to—the beautiful lass and the young boy by her side.

For as the spell had begun, Eoghanan expected to arrive back on the shore of McMillan Castle's lake in precisely the same year that he'd left—1647. Instead he'd landed in a frightening and very noisy jungle filled with tall structures and foul smells. Thankfully, he woke in the shadows and went unnoticed, free to observe the oddities so foreign from all that he'd known.

Pushing thoughts of the experience aside for a moment, he returned to the conversation at hand. "Aye, I doona wish to meet death any time soon. I do wish, however, that ye'd silenced me long enough to warn me of what I would see. I'd like to think that I am no a man easily frightened, but arriving in a place so different from what I expected..." His lack of comprehension stopped him, "was...verra unsettling. But never mind. Tell me about the magic, for if ye doona keep sending me to the same lass, why is it that I end up in her presence each time?"

Morna sat quietly for a moment. Eoghanan assumed she wondered how best to try to explain it to him. Eventually, she spoke. "Do ye remember the stone that brought ye here?"

He nodded, though the memory was a vague one. There'd not been much life in him when he traveled forward. "Aye, I do. What of it?"

"That stone is verra much me own magic. Created by me for the use of yer sister-in-law Mitsy, and now for yerself. But the stone is tied directly to one location and time—yer own. I know enough of how the time travel works and what it does to one's body, essentially ripping ye fair apart before placing ye back together, to know that yer wounds were no healed enough to take ye all the way back that many centuries. I thought it best to use spells already in place for many years, created by others with magic, to allow ye to build up yer strength before such a long travel. They allow me to decide just how far back I wish ye to go, but there are powers greater than me own that choose just exactly where ye end up."

Eoghanan's brows pulled in, displaying his doubt before he had a chance to mask it. "And just what powers are these?"

"I suppose everyone thinks of such a power differently. Ye could call it fate, I suppose. Perhaps, ye are meant to know the lass?"

"No, though she is a lovely sight to be sure, I willna be here long enough to know anyone, save ye and yer husband, Jerry."

Morna said nothing, merely reaching back to grab the cloth, rinsing it once more before gesturing to him to lay back again. "Let me tell ye now, so that there will be no more questions about me being truthful with ye, how I plan to build up yer strength. The first time I sent ye back was to nearly three months ago, and it was too far for yer first trip. This last time was doable, only a week back, but as it still caused ye some pain, I think it best if today's journey only takes ye back a few hours—a day at the most. Tomorrow we shall go a bit farther, a week and a half, I reckon, and then the next day a bit shorter, and so on and so on. One day far, one day close, until we build up yer strength. Is this acceptable to ye?"

Eoghanan winced as the cloth touched his tender skin once more, his voice slightly unsteady as he answered, "Aye, 'tis fine."

Morna smiled at him, squeezing his hand in sympathy before pressing the rag against him once more. "I'm only just to yer shoulder and, after I've cleansed ye, I still have to apply the salve. Best ye tell me about this lass ye have seen. Ye havena spoken of her until today."

"Verra well." He'd thought of nothing else but her for days, so despite Morna's request, it seemed the only natural thing to speak of. Besides, he'd not yet been given the opportunity to write about her and all he'd seen, a practice he'd kept religiously since childhood. He very much didn't want to forget her. Perhaps speaking of the lass would keep her fresh in his memory so that he would have the words ready when it came time to write. "I doona know her name, for each time the wee boy, her son I suppose, calls her 'Mom.' 'Tis no her real name. The lad is called, Cooper. An odd name to be sure, but it seems to fit the lad just fine."

Once he started, the words left him freely, and he took his time describing every instant, recalling every word he'd heard between them. He no longer spoke directly to Morna, but more to himself. It stirred something inside him, to speak of the lass and her son, something that made him feel alive and whole, rather than the weak, wounded man he'd felt like for the past many moons.

The memories of his beloved strangers took him away. He no longer felt the witch's work, not noticing that she'd finished until he heard Jerry's voice in the doorway.

"Morna dear, when ye are finished with him, will ye join me? I need some help in the garden, if ye doona mind. There's a wee beasty weed that is near strangling the life out of one of me plants. I'd like ye to use a bit of magic and kill the devil."

Patting his hand in a motherly fashion, Morna stood from her place beside him, glancing over her shoulder to answer her husband. "I'm finished with him. I'll leave him to rest a while, and we will try out another travel this afternoon."

Eoghanan shifted his eyes from Jerry back to Morna as she addressed him before leaving.

"Are ye comfortable? Will ye be okay for a few hours?"

Eoghanan nodded confidently. "Aye, but I'd like to write in me book. Could ye hand it to me?"

Morna started in the direction of his journal but stopped midway, turning a mischevious smile at him. "No, I doona think so. Ye need to start building yer strength here as well, and walking across the room willna rip ye open from temple to toe. I'll leave ye to get it for yerself."

* * *

Jerry grasped at Morna's arm as soon as she closed the bedroom door behind her. "Ye are much too good at making up lies, love. It unsettles me a bit."

Morna looked at him incredulously. "I doona know what ye mean by that."

He stopped and faced her, blocking her path down the hallway, staring at her with one wiry eyebrow raised, waiting to speak again until she smiled guiltily. "Ach, look there. See, ye do know perfectly what I mean. Ye told the lad that ye doona choose where he ends up. If that were true, I wouldna have had to speak to a Mr. Perdie in America about the money that we will give him to get the lass here, would I?"

"Have ye taken to spying on me, Jerry?"

"I've always spied on ye. Ye get yerself in far too much trouble without me supervision. But I doona believe I knew until today just how well ye could lie."

His wife leaned in to kiss him reassuringly on the cheek. "Life isna worth it without some trouble now and then, but ye shouldna be surprised that I am a good liar. 'Tis a trait of women and the fault of men that we must be so. The folly of ye all has required it of us. I dare ye to find one woman that isna capable of it."

Giving his cheek a quick pat, Morna pushed past him, moving down the hallway ahead of him, leaving Jerry rather stunned and open-mouthed.

Chapter 3

An hour spent in line at airport security, mixed with the general hectic chaos of the airport, was enough to damper the anticipation of even the most enthusiastic traveler. For all his excitement, Cooper had mellowed dramatically from the bouncy, ecstatic boy he'd been this morning by the time we finally sat down at our gate to await boarding.

"Are you nervous?" I nudged him lightly with my elbow, eliciting a trademark lift of an eyebrow as he squirmed in his seat to face me.

"Nah. Why would I be nervous? I've always wanted to fly. I was born to fly, Mama."

I chuckled, glancing down at my watch to check the time. "Oh you were, huh? Well, you'll get to shortly. Only an hour until take off now. I bet we start boarding within the next fifteen minutes or so."

"Fifteen?" For a brief second his voice held a slight whine, but he checked it quickly, knowing it wouldn't be tolerated. "I don't think I can even last another five." He held up four fingers, but silently counted as he looked over his hand and quickly extended his thumb so it displayed the correct number.

"Oh, I bet you can. Let's do something to pass the time. Want to work on your reading?" He loved for me to read to him and, no surprise, he was catching on quickly.

Enthused, he immediately reached to the floor to grab his backpack so that he could pick a reading choice.

"Can we read the book Dad gave me last night?"

"Sure." I responded reflexively, but I watched him

rummage through his bag apprehensively. Jeffrey was in no way much of a reader. I couldn't, for the life of me, imagine Jeffrey going to a bookstore to find a book for Cooper. I anticipated him pulling a comic out of his backpack. That was fine. It just wouldn't be the reading material I knew Cooper would want. He didn't enjoy pop-up and sticker books; he wanted more words than pictures. Just another trait that made him anything but the typical child.

"This one."

Surprising me, he extended *The Little Prince* by Antoine deSaint Exupery. So much more than a simplistic children's story, this tale had just the sort of depth that Cooper would enjoy, although I would have to explain some of the meaning to him, he wouldn't mind. He loved to learn.

"Dad gave this to you?" I couldn't mask the doubt in my voice.

"Yeah, but Bebop helped. He said that since the two of you were getting so many gifts for the wedding, I needed something too. He said he didn't know what to get me, but then Bebop helped."

That made much more sense. It was Cooper's Bebop, Jeffrey's dad, who'd introduced me to the story when I'd been a little girl. A warm, funny, and caring man so different from my own father, I spent most of my childhood wishing I'd been born to him instead.

"Ah, well this is a very special gift, ya know? It's one of my favorites."

"Really?" I'd drawn him in now. Knowing that I loved the book, he'd sit contently and listen to me read it, even if he didn't care for it, although I knew he would.

"Yes, really. Scoot in closer and I'll start. I don't think this is the best book for us to practice your own reading with though, it's a bit long."

He pulled his feet up into the seat and slid in tight, leaning toward me. "That's fine. I'll just listen."

He smiled, leaning his head against my shoulder as my heart squeezed happily. I'd just opened the cover when we were interrupted by an attendant alerting all those at our gate that boarding would begin promptly.

"Ope!" I made the excited noise as I closed the spine and slid the book back into his backpack. "This is it, Coop. We'll read it on the plane, okay?"

"Okay."

His legs flew off the seat so fast, he just about fell down, but catching himself he threw his backpack on and smiled ecstatically, as happy as I'd ever seen him.

Thrilled as he was, he flatly refused to board with the group "travelers with small children." While I would've enjoyed the benefit of getting on the plane first, I didn't push the issue. I wouldn't put a damper on anything that brought him this much joy.

So once all pre-boarders had entered, we lined up with the rest, squished firmly somewhere in between groups B and C. He held my hand tightly, leaning out past the line so that he could see something besides the backsides of those in front of us.

I watched him smiling, when suddenly he jerked away from me, spinning to face something catty-corner from the line where he waved a little shyly. Startled, I crouched down next to him, placing my hand on his shoulder so that I could steady myself while I looked in the same direction. I could see no one—no one that either of us knew at least.

"What are you waving at?" I lightly squeezed his shoulder to pull his attention away from who or whatever he looked at so intently.

"Over there." He pointed to the side of an escalator, where a shadow spread deep over the tile around it. "Do you remember the man I told you about at the park? With the scars? He's here again."

Grateful that I'd steadied myself with his shoulder, I spun

him toward me, doing my best to keep my voice calm despite the shiver that shook me all over. "I remember you mentioning the man, but I never saw him. Are you sure he's here now?"

I released my grip so that he could turn and look again and I tried to do the same. Again, I saw no one. Cooper refaced me, clearly frustrated. "He's not there anymore, but he was, I know it."

Cooper didn't lie. Even when he tried to, he could only last a few seconds before his face would give way with guilt and he would fess up. If he believed he saw someone, he meant it, but why had I not noticed him?

Sure, I had a lot on my mind lately—my almost wedding and new job—not to mention that, like every mother, half of my mind always rested on Cooper. Still, it seemed that every time I made to look at the man Cooper mentioned, the stranger vanished into thin air. I couldn't help but wonder if Cooper saw someone who wasn't really there. An imaginary friend, perhaps? As the line started to move, I decided to direct my questioning to that effect.

"So, what's your new friend's name?"

He looked up at me with a face that plainly meant he thought I'd lost my mind. "I don't know him, Mom. I don't know his name."

He shook his head at me, apparently astonished at my stupidity.

"Well, then why did you wave at him?"

He shrugged, lifting my hand a little. "He looked sad and he looked right at me, just like at the park."

The thought made me uneasy. "You said he has bad scars? Does he scare you?"

"No." He seemed surprised by my suggestion. "He's not a bad guy just because he has scars, Mom."

"Of course not," I muttered quickly. Instantly regretting the implication of my question. "I just meant," *what did I mean?* "He's a stranger. How do you know he's not scary?"

21

He shrugged his little shoulders and we stepped forward a step in the line. "Bebop says even if somebody is smiling, you can see meanness in their eyes." He paused a moment and I said nothing, knowing by his held breath that he wasn't finished speaking. "And I think he's right. Just look at Grandfather. He smiles at people all the time, but he's not very nice."

I looked down at him, unsure of what to say. It seemed wrong to let him speak poorly of my father, but I could hardly disagree with him. Instead, I chose to direct the conversation back to the stranger. "So this man's eyes weren't mean, huh?"

"Nope. I think he likes us, Mom."

We neared the gate and I extended Cooper's boarding pass toward him so that he could hand it to the attendant to scan. "Well, why wouldn't he like us? Here—do you want to hand it to her?"

"Yes!" He snatched it from me excitedly and leaned to the side to see how close we were to the front. "We're almost there, we're almost there. You can let go of my hand now too if you want, Mom."

I released his hand, stepping behind him so that he could have his ticket checked first. After both our tickets were scanned, I stayed a half-step behind him, allowing him to lead us into the makeshift hallway leading toward the plane. He all but bounced up and down with the excitement that radiated off him.

His happiness did me good and, for a moment, I forgot all about Cooper's mysterious stranger until a quick glance down at my bag made me realize I'd left my jacket draped over the chair where Cooper and I had been sitting.

Calling to him to stop, I waved him toward me. "Hey, I want you to wait right here. I left my coat, I'm just going to go ask the attendant if she'll grab it for me."

He nodded, trying to hide his disappointment that we would move back a few places in the line to get on the plane.

Squeezing his hand, I stepped away and hurried back up the ramp, pushing my way against the flow of people until I stood next to the gate entry, being sure not to step back outside of it. "Miss…" I reached out to tap the girl on the shoulder. "I'm so sorry, I believe I left my jacket on that chair over there." I pointed in the direction of the chair, but couldn't see it due to the line. "Would you mind grabbing it for me?"

To my surprise, she extended the light cotton jacket in my direction. "Is it this one?"

"Why, yes." I reached out for it, surprised it had been noticed amongst the crowd of people. "Did a passenger pick it up?"

She shook her head and jerked it to the side, "Not a passenger on this plane. He must have been waiting at another gate. He just laid it over the counter here and turned to walk away before I could speak to him."

"Which way did he go?" I looked around the mass of people, trying to find the man I suspected.

"I don't know. I'm a bit busy, as you can see."

The woman smiled, but clearly she wished for me to leave now. Although there was no way for me to know for sure, Cooper's stranger was, once again, very much on my mind.

Chapter 4

Overnight flights are meant to be slept on but, try as I might to explain this concept to Cooper, he had none of it. While he still operated with the same inexhaustible amount of energy he had aboard the flight, the full effects of jet lag crashed down on me hard, making me ill-tempered.

"Mr. Perdie, there's no way this is where I'm supposed to stay. I know you said it was an inn, but there's no sign or anything. It's in the middle of nowhere. Why on earth would an inn set up here?"

I fumbled with the GPS system with one hand, holding my phone to my ear with the other. While Perdie read aloud the coordinates, I frowned down at the navigation screen in frustration. "Yes, that's exactly where I am but this...this just can't be it."

"Mom, look!"

His voice, loud, high, and demanding sounded as pleasing to my tired ears as an out of tune oboe. "Coop," I snapped a little too harshly. "What have I told you about when I'm on the phone? You have to wait until I'm finished."

"But…" his voice quivered but he continued, determined to be heard. "There's a man at the door. He's wav...waving." His voice broke completely as he finished and my heart with it.

I hurried off the phone with Mr. Perdie, mumbling something along the lines of, "Never mind, I'll call you later," before making haste to apologize. "I'm sorry. I shouldn't have yelled at you. I'm just exhausted. No sleep turns me into a scary troll."

"A very scary troll," he said.

Although he wasn't ready to smile at me, I knew I'd been forgiven. "Now, what's this about a man? I don't see anybody." *Again,* I thought to myself. It worried me that twice in the course of twenty-four hours Cooper had seen someone I hadn't. Although, I wasn't sure which one of us I should be worried for—him for his overactive imagination or myself for my horrifying lack of observational skills. I guess we would find out soon enough.

Cooper threw his hands up in exasperation. "Well, that's because he went back inside." He waved real big and then," he pulled his hand toward his chest, demonstrating the man's hand motion, "he wants us to come inside, too."

After putting the car back in drive long enough so that I could turn off the main road and park in front of the inn, I turned off the engine. "Alright. I'll take your word for it. Let's leave our bags here, just in case, okay?"

Unbuckling his seat belt, he nodded before reaching to open the car door, popping the handle with his fingers and then kicking it open the rest of the way with his feet. Once outside, he slammed the door as hard as he could, which was just hard enough to close the door back properly.

Anxious to greet the man who'd waved to him, Cooper knocked on the front door before I reached his side. As I neared him, the door swung open, revealing an ancient-looking man who for a moment, however brief, looked so grumpy that I could scarcely imagine that this was the man Cooper thought had waved us inside.

Much to my astonishment, the stranger's face altered completely in the next second, transforming with a smile so large and warm that the vast contrast to how he appeared only a moment ago would have unsettled me in most cases, but the old man now appeared so welcoming that both Cooper and I couldn't help but smile in return.

He extended a large, bony hand and Cooper reached out confidently to grasp it firmly—perhaps the one good thing my father had taught him.

"Why, good morning, lad. We've been expecting ye. I am Jerry. I believe that me wife has prepared some brunch for ye both. Why doona ye come in?" The man looked up at me and smiled before returning his attention to Cooper. "And who might this lovely lass standing behind ye be?"

Cooper reached his left hand behind him, extending it in my direction so that I would take it, effectively presenting me to the man. When he wished to be, Coop had it in him to be quite the little gentleman.

"This is my Mom."

The man, Jerry, stepped forward. I moved to extend my own hand, but instead he clasped me on the shoulder, ushering us inside. "Aye, I reckoned she was, though she looks young enough to be yer sister. What is yer name, laddie, and how old are ye?"

Continuing to move down the hall in the direction Jerry indicated, Cooper occasionally glanced behind him so that he could look at Jerry as he spoke. "Cooper and I'm four years old, but not really four because I'll be five very soon."

"Ach, I'd have guessed ye a fair deal older than that, laddie."

Cooper nodded, clearly expecting this response. "Yeah, everybody says that."

"And ye…" Jerry lowered his voice so that I knew he now spoke to me and not Cooper, "must be Grace, aye?"

I nodded, battling a brief moment of confusion. The reservation must have required something more than the name of the magazine for him to know my first name. I knew for certain I hadn't been given the chance to introduce myself yet.

We stepped into the kitchen and, while the smell was enough to alert us that someone had been busy cooking, the room was empty. Still, Jerry ushered us inside.

"Go on and have a seat, the both of ye. I believe me wife has stepped upstairs to invite our other guest down for a meal, though he usually dines in his room, I expect he'd like to meet the two of ye."

"Why?" I asked the question before I had a chance to check it, but I didn't understand his conclusion. If I were staying at an inn, I certainly wouldn't feel the need to meet and greet every new guest that checked in.

"Ach, well," the old man seemed slightly rattled by my question, or perhaps, the bluntness of it. "He's been here several months now, and the two of ye are the first guests we've had since he arrived. I expect me wife thinks 'twould do him good to see some other people."

"Don't you think a grown man can decide for himself what would do him good? Why has he been here so long? It certainly doesn't look like there would be much to do around here." I surprised myself once again with another question. Usually, I wasn't this blunt, but something about this situation and the conversation at present felt very odd to me, and I couldn't help but continue my inquiry.

"Why, lass, I just offered ye food. Why ye feel the need to berate me so, I doona know. Both of yer questions ye can ask the lad yerself when he gets down here. Now, sit."

He pointed at a chair to his left. I did as he bid, ashamed at my lack of manners. "I'm sorry. I'm afraid jet-lag is hitting me rather hard. I appreciate the food. We both do."

Jerry patted and squeezed my shoulder once again. "Doona worry about it, lass. Travel is a tough business. Ye two help yerself to the food. I'll go see if me wife needs some help."

He slipped quickly away. Before I could gather the energy to stand, I glanced over to see Cooper standing on his tiptoes in an effort to reach the eggs on the stove, just nearly about to dump them right onto the floor.

Leaping from my seat, I pulled on the last of my energy reserves to reach for the tilting plate.

* * *

"How do ye feel, lad?"

Morna's voice next to his bedside worried Eoghanan. Perhaps the travel had injured him this time, though as he lay with his eyes closed, he felt no more pain than usual. Each time the journey made his head ache and his wounds burn, but all in all, he seemed in less pain than the previous times.

He jerked his eyes open, adjusting to the bright light above him, working to collect himself from the slight confusion that followed each journey before finally looking in Morna's direction.

"I feel better than before, though me head aches as it always does."

"Aye, I'm afraid there's no way around that bit of it. Do ye feel like rising from yer bed for a while? We have new visitors who will be staying with us. I think it polite if ye come and meet them. Ye are bound to bump into one another over the next few weeks."

Her words surprised him. Not a soul had happened across his host's home since his arrival. So many days spent in near solitude made him doubt his ability to communicate suitably, especially if the visitors were from the time he found himself in now. "No, thank ye, Morna. I think it best that I rest a while more."

The look on Morna's face confirmed his fears. She'd not meant it as a real question and threw a wad of strange clothes on him. "I dinna ask ye for ye to say 'no'. Now, ye can either get up, or I shall drag ye up, but downstairs to the kitchen ye shall go one way or the other."

Resigned, Eoghanan slowly swung his legs over the side of the bed, sitting up. Thankfully, the task of moving about normally became easier with each passing day. "Fine. I dinna think ye would let me stay here, but I thought it worth a try."

"Ye knew it fruitless to try before ye uttered the words. Now put these on. Ye canna wear the loose linen ye have on now, for no man would wear it in this time. I have tried to find ye the lightest modern material I could, so it willna press too much against yer side, but no doubt ye will feel it against the scar."

Eoghanan held up both garments. The first, while about the length of a kilt, was made of a fabric he'd never seen before and had two holes, one for each of his legs, he assumed. The top scrunched together and, as he pulled on the sides, he watched in fascination as the bottoms grew and shrunk with his efforts. "And what are these, Morna?"

"I believe that American men wear them while they play sports. Jerry said he's seen basketball players don them. I thought that since the waistband is moveable, it would hurt less than placing ye in a pair of fitted pants."

Eoghanan frowned down at the garments. "Men must take no pride in how they look to wear such ridiculous garments. Can I no just wear me kilt?"

"It's too heavy just yet. It would rub right against yer scars. Just strip yer clothes, and I'll help ye. Doona be shy about it either. All these months of healing ye, I've seen every blessed inch of ye, and ye know it well."

Not a skilled talker on his best day, Eoghanan knew the witch would win every war of words with him. So he stood to step out of the thin linen pants, deciding not to argue the point further. His mind took him, instead, back to where he'd been only moments before. "The lad saw me this time. I know he did. I suspected he did the first time, but I couldna be sure. This time though, he waved at me."

He thought back on the boy, smiling and waving at him as if he'd known him all his young life.

"Oh?" Morna's voice spoke as she lifted his foot to slide into a solid white, strange foot covering she called a 'tennis-shoe.' "I'll no say that it surprises me that a child was the one to see ye. They are much more perceptive than adults."

"Aye, I believe the boy to be verra wise for his small age. He dinna seem to be afraid of the way I look." Eoghanan tried to wiggle his toes, grimacing at the monstrosity being strapped to his foot.

"Why would he be? Ye look mighty fine in me eyes, and I'd be hard pressed to find any lass that dinna think ye so."

He pulled up one corner of his mouth in disagreement. "Mayhap once, but no so much anymore. I doona mind it, but 'tis true well enough."

"Hogwash," Morna swatted his covered foot dismissively. "Yer scars may look a bit painful now, but as they fade, they will only draw lassies to ye, wait and see. Makes ye look a wee bit dangerous, and I doona know any lass that doesna like a bit of danger whether she is willing to admit it or no. No matter that ye are about as dangerous as a wee kitten, ye willna look that way, and that's what matters."

"If ye say so. Are ye done with me? I feel rather foolish."

In answer to his question, Morna stood from her crouching place at his feet. "Aye. Ye know ye seemed surprised that the child wasna scared of the way ye looked. Children are only afraid of what they're taught to be afraid of." She paused and opened the bedroom door, motioning toward him so that he would follow her into the hallway. "'Tis a credit to the boy's mother that he wasna bothered by ye. It means she's taught him to look at more than how a person looks."

Mention of the lad's mother, as he followed Morna down the stairs and into the hallway, made Eoghanan think back to the way her garment felt in his hands and the risk he'd taken by going after it once she'd left it. It smelled lovely, as if he were holding her in his arms. He almost wished to keep it for himself but instead had left it for her, quickly rushing back to his place in the shadows. He could almost smell it now, the same scent he'd noticed on the covering. The fragrance so lifelike in his memory, he found himself bewildered by it. How could he smell something so strongly when it wasn't there?

He stepped into the kitchen to greet the inn's new guests and stopped still. The scent that lingered in his memory instead clung to the very woman he thought of. She stood before him now, both she and the young lad.

Chapter 5

"Hey, I know you. Did you get on the same plane as us?"

I'd just sat Cooper down at the kitchen table with a plate full of eggs and some sort of weird sausage I had no intention of eating when Cooper's exclamation caused me to glance up to where Jerry's wife, along with the inn's other resident, appeared in the doorway.

I understood Cooper's words immediately upon looking at the man, and the room suddenly seemed to grow quite small. I reached behind to steady myself but found that I groped at nothing but air until Jerry's knowing hand found mine as he stepped to my side. "Are ye alright, lass?"

I nodded as Jerry led me to a chair next to Cooper. He spoke up on my behalf.

"She's just a bit tired is all. Verra long trip from America. I think some sleep would do her good."

"Well, she canna sleep yet. Her inner clock would be totally awry if she were to sleep now. She must at least make it through the day before resting." Jerry's wife stepped toward me in greeting, placing her hand on my shoulder, much as Jerry had done. "I'm Morna, I'll get ye some coffee."

I said nothing to her as I continued to stare at the man who remained in the doorway. Scars or no, this couldn't have been the man Cooper believed he'd seen. The attendant had said herself the man wasn't on our flight. Even if he had been, how could he have beaten us here? We'd been shuttled straight from the airport to the car rental and come straight from the car rental here. Besides, Jerry had said this man had been a guest at the inn for months.

Allowing myself to rationalize the man's presence and Cooper's reaction to him as a simple case of mistaken identity, I allowed myself to look him over without such a sense of overwhelming alarm. Much like the stranger Cooper spoke of, I found nothing about this man's appearance frightening, although intimidating was another matter entirely.

Despite his ridiculous outfit of stark white tennis shoes, socks that went halfway up his calves, black athletic shorts, and a simple white undershirt, he exuded such confident masculinity it made something within my veins hum to life with awareness of him. He filled the width of the doorway with his wide shoulders and was tall enough to have to crouch underneath it. I imagined he stood at least six feet five and, despite being quite lean in stature, I guessed him to weigh a good two hundred and sixty pounds—all muscle.

His eyes were shockingly green, highlighted by specks of gold that seemed to reflect light in a way that made his eyes stand out amongst the mass of red hair that reached his shoulders. His state of dress made little sense to me; there was such a raw manliness to him, a note of pride and refinement to the way he carried himself that I couldn't imagine him wearing such a laid-back outfit on a day-to-day basis.

Only when I tore my gaze away from his eyes and focused on the scar that ran from the top of his temple on his right side, all the way down to the top of his sock, did I understand the garb. He didn't bear the scars of an old wound but a new one. They were still fresh—pink and angry in their appearance, still soft and, I supposed, very much still sore.

Cooper's voice startled me, and I glanced down at the plate Morna placed in front of me with embarrassment. I'd unapologetically been staring the man down, most likely the last thing he needed after whatever horrible thing had happened to him to cause such a wound.

"Hey, mister, didn't you hear what I said? Did you come here on the same plane? What's your name?"

I glanced up from my plate with reddened cheeks and watched the man's reaction to my son closely. He too seemed to have to pull himself away from something. Only then did I realize that he'd been studying me just as closely as I had him.

He coughed into a clenched fist seemingly to find his voice and took a step into the kitchen, pulling himself up to his full height for the first time. Looking at Cooper, he shook his head and smiled. "No, I dinna. Me name is Eoghanan. What shall I call ye, lad?"

Cooper beamed at the oddity of the man's name. Pushing himself away from the table, he stood and approached the man who towered over him.

"Yo-yu-what? My name is Cooper."

He stuck his hand out toward the man who took it gladly, allowing Cooper to shake it for far longer than was customary. At least the man seemed to have patience when it came to children. That said something about his character.

The man announced his name again, only a little more slowly, making it sound even more unusual. Cooper couldn't refrain from giggling.

"I've never heard a name like that before. Yo-yun...yo-yun.." Cooper fumbled with the strange syllables before finally throwing his hands up in exasperation. "I give up. How about I just call you E-o? Would that be okay?"

E-o, as my son renamed him, let loose a smile so bright that it seemed to ease some of the tension in the room before his deep laughter made everyone smile in curious wonderment at what he found so funny.

Cooper seemed especially intent on finding out. "What's so funny? I just gave you a nickname is all. Lots of people have those. Mine is Coop. Mama calls me that a lot. You can call me that if you want to, too. That, or just Cooper, I don't mind either one."

Now free from my son's handshake, Eoghanan moved across the room to fill his own plate, speaking with his back toward us as he did so. "'Tis only that yer 'nickname' as ye called it, made me think of someone verra dear. She too has trouble with me name and decided on the same name as ye have, lad. And aye, ye may call me E-o for I know she wouldna mind sharing it with ye."

With his plate full, he joined us at the table, sitting next to Morna and across from me and Cooper with Jerry rounding out the table by sitting at its head. The table was smaller than what one would find at the average restaurant. As a result, the five of us found ourselves sitting in very close proximity. No matter that most of us were strangers to one another, I found it impossible to behave that way with the familiar way in which we sat, and I unthinkingly blurted out the first thing that came to mind.

"The woman who called you by the same name—was she a girlfriend? Or an ex-wife perhaps?" The questions slipped out, and I groaned internally. It was absolutely none of my business. Apparently, lack of sleep had the remarkable ability to loosen my tongue. It no longer seemed safe for me to be in the presence of those I might insult, and decided it time that Cooper and I leave to explore the area for the rest of the day— just as soon as we finished our meal.

With an even deeper blush than before, I raised my eyes to see a look of amusement on the man's face.

"I doona believe that I know yer name, lass."

"I...I'm sorry. It's. I'm Grace." I sat down my fork and held out a hand in between stuttered words. He took my fingertips into his hand, kissing my knuckles before pulling away and directing his attention back to his food.

"'Tis a pleasure to meet ye, Grace. Aye, the lass is the bonniest of girlfriends. Can one have an ex-wife as ye said? I doona know, but she is no me wife. She is me brother's."

"Ah." The noise made little sense, but neither did his explanation. Either he didn't understand what a girlfriend was, or he'd just gleefully confessed to sleeping with his sister-in-law. And to my knowledge there were few places left in the world that didn't acknowledge some sort of spousal separation. Perhaps it was his way of making some sort of joke I didn't get. I very much hoped he wasn't a comedian.

Not wishing to delve further into that can of worms, I finished my food as quickly as possible and waited patiently for Cooper to do the same. Once he'd clearly had his fill, I stood scooping up both our plates so that I could rinse them, only stopping at Morna's insistence.

"If ye know what's best for ye, lass, ye will leave those dishes be right this instant. No guest of mine will ever clean a dish if I have anything to say about it. Why doona ye go with Jerry, and he'll help ye carry yer bags to yer room and allow ye some time to settle in?"

Obeying, I left the dishes inside the sink, turning so that I could properly address her. "Thank you, but I think we'll wait to get our bags if that's alright? I'd like to go ahead and scope out the lay of the land and decide just what I want to work on photographing tomorrow."

Morna stood as Cooper hopped down from his seat to make his way over to me. "Aye, o'course. The two of ye are free to do as ye wish."

"Okay, great. We will be back sometime this afternoon. Thank you for the food. It was delicious." I reached to rub my fingers through Cooper's hair as he approached me. "Wasn't it, Coop? You ready?"

"Yep, but can I ask E-o one question first?"

A scary question coming from someone as inquisitive as Cooper, but I didn't imagine there was much chance of him asking something as intrusive as I had done. "I don't mind, but it's up to him whether or not he answers your question."

Eoghanan smiled, clearly ready to hear what Cooper meant to ask him. "Ask whatever ye wish, lad. I'll answer ye."

"If you didn't come here on the plane with us, did you fly in on a spaceship? 'Cause I know you're the same man I saw at the playground and at the airport." Astonishingly, he didn't smile or laugh as he asked. He meant it as an entirely serious question.

"What? Cooper, why would you ask him that?" I answered in Eoghanan's place, wishing to spare him the oncoming conversation.

"Maybe he's like the little prince in the book, Mom. He flies around to different places like the little prince did to different planets."

"Oh, I see." Realization dawned on me as I remembered our flight time story. At least he was making text-to-world connections, regardless of how far-fetched they might be. "Coop, you know that was just a story, right?"

He twisted where he stood, crossing his arms as he looked up at me, disappointed. "Oh man, Mom. I guess that means you're a real grown-up then. Only a grown-up would say it was just a story. Don't you remember the problem with grown-ups from the book? Kids see things more clearly."

This would require a longer conversation than I was willing to have in front of our captive audience. "Often times they do, Coop, but I don't think your new friend is the same man. We'll talk about it more in a minute. Let's get out of everyone's hair for a bit."

I took a step toward the doorway. Thankfully, Cooper followed.

"Okay, but it doesn't matter what you say, Mom. I know he's the same guy."

I stood waiting for him in the doorway, but he stopped right as he walked past Eoghanan. Spinning on his heels, Cooper faced him and pointed an accusing finger in Eoghanan's direction before he spoke once more.

"I don't know why you're not agreeing with me, sir. I know who I saw and it was you." He emphasized the last word and thrust his finger forward for drama. "If you lie and say you weren't at the park and at the airport, I won't believe you."

Switching his attitude as quickly as one could flip a switch, he spun once more to face Jerry and Morna. "Thanks for the eggs. They were so yummy. See you guys later."

37

With that, he spun a final time, marching past me, down the hall, and out the front door of the inn.

"That's some lad ye have there, Grace." Jerry chuckled as he spoke.

"Yes, quite." I glanced down at my watch, drained in every imaginable way as I took off down the hallway after him. It was only eleven a.m.

Chapter 6

Apparently immune to any symptoms of jetlag, Cooper's energy didn't drag until we finally turned into the inn late that evening, after hours of driving and walking around the Scottish countryside surrounding the oddly placed inn.

Thankfully, I awoke the next morning much more adjusted to the time difference and determined not to be as loose-lipped or grumpy as I'd been the day before.

My resolve lasted for most of the morning but by noon, with too little work completed, I found myself wishing for a daycare that could take Coop off my hands, if only for a few hours. He would've hated every minute of it, but unless he wanted me fired, I thought it a form of torture he could handle for an afternoon—not that there was any daycare to subject him to anyway.

"Coop, if you jump up in front of my camera lens while I'm taking a photo one more time, I am going to unleash the tickle monster."

"Okay...okay. I'll stop." He collapsed onto the lawn in front of me, busying himself by picking at blades of grass. While most children would've antagonized further at the threat of a good tickle, Cooper hated it, and I knew the threat would stop him.

As if in answer to my silent prayer, Cooper jumped up in exclamation at our two approaching visitors, Jerry and Eoghanan. "Look Mom! Look!"

Placing my camera back in its bag, I waved them over, happy to see anyone who would provide Cooper a moment of distraction.

"We come with strict instructions to see the two of ye properly fed." Eoghanan lifted the basket he held in his hands, sitting it on the ground as he neared us.

"Oh thank goodness, I'm starving." Cooper ran toward them, squeezing in between them and grabbing each man's hand as he bounced excitedly between them.

I shook my head as I moved to greet them, "Starving? I'm sure glad I packed those gummy bears before we left. You've just eaten a pound of them."

Once Jerry and Eoghanan stopped walking, Cooper released their hands and stepped toward me. "I would've eaten two pounds if you'd let me."

"I have no doubt. That's why I stopped you." Though thin now, I'd been a chunky kid. I didn't wish Cooper to repeat history.

"What is a 'gummy bear'?" Eoghanan's face twisted with confusion.

I could only hope they called them by a different name in Scotland. Surely, he didn't truly not know what a gummy bear was.

"What? You've never had one? Well, I'll give you one right now." Cooper started to tug on the bag hanging from my shoulder. I relented, reaching inside for the bag of gummies. Once he had them in hand, he extended them to Eoghanan. "You have to try this."

After examining it closely, Eoghanan obliged and popped the gummy in his mouth. Watching him struggle with the texture, I couldn't help but believe he'd never experienced such a food before.

Swallowing the snack with effort, Eoghanan looked down at Cooper to give him his thoughts. "That is…well, that's quite an interesting food, lad."

Cooper nodded, taking his words as confirmation of their deliciousness. "Yeah, I know. They're amazing."

"Thank ye for allowing me one." Eoghanan looked away from Cooper and up at me. "Could I speak with ye alone a moment, Grace?"

His question surprised me, but I nodded and nudged

Cooper toward Jerry. "Coop, help Jerry lay out the blanket and get the food ready, okay?"

"Got it." He smiled over his shoulder as Eoghanan walked off in the other direction.

As we walked, I rolled the top of the bag of gummies closed and started to place them back in my bag before nudging Eoghanan slightly with my elbow, waving the bag in his direction. "Would you like another?" I laughed quietly, knowing his answer even before he spoke.

"Thank ye, but no. I dinna much care for it."

I laughed while placing them back in my bag. "I could tell. Have you really never had them before? Where did you grow up?"

I thought I saw him shift uncomfortably at my question. "No, 'twas me first and last gummy bear. I grew up verra far from here, ye wouldna have heard of it."

He said nothing else, and I didn't press him but stopped walking now that we were far enough away that Cooper and Jerry couldn't hear us. "What did you want to talk to me about?"

Eoghanan stopped walking as well and faced me. "I wished to apologize for upsetting yer son yesterday morn."

"Oh, don't." I interrupted him and reached my hand out, placing it on the side of his arm to silence him. "It's not your fault. He only…he thought you were someone else. Really, you didn't upset him." His face turned suddenly very white. I jerked my hand away, realizing that I'd placed it right along his scar. "I'm so sorry."

He rolled his shoulder a bit in an effort to shake away the pain. "'Tis nothing, lass. Doona worry yerself over it. I wish to ask ye if ye will allow young Cooper to join Jerry and meself this afternoon. We intend to go fishing."

His thoughtfulness in asking me away from Cooper, in case I said no, meant a great deal to me. He didn't wish to get Cooper's hopes up if I wouldn't allow it and didn't want to place me in an uncomfortable situation by pushing my hand. It was the act of a gentleman, and he instantly gained my trust by doing so.

"Honestly, it would be great to have a few hours of uninterrupted work. If Cooper wants to go, I have no problem with it as long as you stay near the inn and you take care of my son."

"Aye, I suspected ye might need time alone to tend to yer work." He took one step toward the direction we'd come, indicating that we could begin our walk back.

As I moved next to him, he placed a hand on the small of my back and leaned in close. It seemed slightly intimate, but I was oddly comfortable with him and I didn't move away as he spoke.

"And I promise ye, Grace, I'll return Cooper safely back to ye."

Eoghanan was still very much a stranger to me, but I believed him. He didn't seem like the type of man who would say anything he didn't mean. "I know," I muttered as we neared the others and stepped away from one another.

* * *

"Ye are verra talented at catching the wee fish, Cooper." Eoghanan pulled the fish off its hook, tossing it back into the water to freedom.

"Yep, but I been fishin' a long time." Cooper patted him comfortingly on the shoulder. "You'll get the hang of it. Just takes practice."

Eoghanan laughed, placing another piece of bait on the rod so that Cooper could cast it into the water once again. "No, lad, I doona think me fishing will improve. The wee beasties doona like me. Who taught ye to fish?"

"My BeBop."

"What is a BeBop?" Eoghanan found the names in this century no stranger than his own.

"That's my grandfather's name. Hey, do you want a gummy? You look kinda tired or something. I think I have two more left in my pocket."

The thought of another tiny yellow or blue creature entering his mouth made Eoghanan swallow hard to wash away the lingering taste before answering. "I am tired, but why doona ye eat both of them? I doona think I'm verra hungry just now."

Cooper waved the two bears temptingly in front of him. "You sure?"

"Aye, I'm verra sure."

Smiling, the child dusted off a piece of lint from one of the gummies that had been in his pocket before he popped them both into his mouth, closing his eyes as he chewed.

Watching Cooper enjoy his mouthful, Eoghanan stood and walked over to Jerry who lay napping in the sun.

"Jerry, I think it best we make our way back. I need to do a travel with Morna, and I'd like to be back before the evening meal."

"Huh?" The old man jerked up from lying horizontally on the ground, his back cracking as he sat up. "What did ye say, lad?"

"I'm sorry, I dinna wish to wake ye. 'Tis only I think we should go so that I can do me travel with Morna."

"Ah, verra right." Jerry held his hand out for assistance. "Ye must help me up though, or I'll be here all night. I doona have the same knees I once did."

"Up ye go."

He reached toward the old man with his left hand, being sure not to strain the other half of his body too much as he lifted him. Seeing Jerry rightly vertical, he hollered after Cooper.

"Have ye had yer fill of fishing? If so, I think it time to go. Yer mother shall be back at the inn soon enough."

Mention of the boy's mother had Cooper gathering up his

rod and tools as quickly as his little arms could move to reach them. While Eoghanan knew the boy had enjoyed their afternoon, he didn't wish to be away from his mother for long. He didn't blame him in the slightest and found himself ready to be in Grace's presence once again as well.

* * *

"I know we must make a journey daily, but do ye mind making it a verra short one? I wish to be back before Grace returns from her work."

"Oh, do ye now? I expected ye to say as much. Aye, verra short. Now, lay back so that I may begin."

He did as she asked, placing his left hand behind his head to prop himself up a little as Morna began her spell. As always, his head began to split first, the pain shooting down his spine and shaking him all over. Vision blurred quickly but, just before he evaporated entirely, he caught movement in the doorway and directed his focus just long enough to see Cooper peering inside with wide eyes.

Chapter 7

"Oh. My. Jiminy. Cricket. That is sooo much cooler than a spaceship! It's magic, huh? You used magic on him. Where did he go?"

Cooper's voice filled the room, and Eoghanan struggled against the fog consuming his brain to stay present. He no longer wished to make a travel today, not now that the boy had seen him. Why wouldn't Morna cease her spell? She saw the boy but continued her low chant, sending him further into oblivion.

Speech eluded him. He couldn't answer Cooper with his physical body already gone from the room. Only his hearing and sight remained, although his vision remained blurred. He could hear Cooper's voice calling after Morna, but he couldn't see the room clearly, only making out the faint edges of the young lad and the witch.

Morna's words grew louder and with it his consciousness weakened. He couldn't be certain, but Morna's words seemed to change, different from the ones she usually spoke. Suddenly everything went black.

* * *

In the next instant, he was back in the room, his eyelids fluttering open to find Cooper sitting on the bed next to him, his little hands cupping both sides of his cheeks.

"Wake up, sleepy. I knew it, E-o. I knew you were the same person that was in the park and at the airport. You're magic!"

His head throbbed even worse than usual, but he pushed the pain aside, attributing it to the fact that his journey had been interrupted. He couldn't tell how long he'd been out, but he'd not arrived anywhere in the past. He simply remained in the space between until Morna called him back to the present.

Eoghanan propped himself up in the bed as Cooper released his face. Looking around the room for Morna, he addressed her first. "How long was I gone?"

The witch made her way to him, extending a cool rag to press along his forehead. "Ach, no more than a few minutes. The second the lad walked into the room, I started the return spell. I'm only pleased that all of ye arrived back here."

"Ye dinna know if I would?" The notion unsettled him. The travels were frightening enough without worrying about the possibility of his legs ending up in one century and his head in another.

"No, I couldna know for sure. This has never happened before."

"Did ye tell him?" Eoghanan glanced over at Cooper who nodded emphatically at his question.

"Yes, she did. I know everything. She's a witch and you're from like a million years ago. It's awesome!"

Morna shut the door to the bedroom so that the three of them could speak more freely. "Aye, I dinna have a choice. I doona believe he would have ever silenced if I hadna done so. But ye needn't worry, I shall make him forget it. I was just waiting for you to wake up first."

"No way." Cooper kept his voice calm, but reached out latching hard onto Eoghanan's hand. "Don't you let her put those witchy hands on me, E-o. I won't tell anybody. I promise."

Morna laughed in response, waving a hand in dismissal. "Doona worry, lad. I willna place a hand on ye. I'm no bad witch, surely ye can see that. I'll just say a few words, and ye willna know that ye are missing the memory."

"No." Eoghanan spoke, settling the matter in his mind. He trusted Morna completely, but it didn't mean he wished her to use magic on the lad. If knowing that magic truly existed in the world would bring the boy joy, he didn't wish to take it from him.

"Ye know that we doona have a choice, Eoghanan." Morna reached to take the rag from him, walking across the room to hang it over the basin.

"Aye, we do. Ye have told me yerself that too few people know of the existence of magic in this present world. Now that the lad knows, doona rob him of it. I believe we can trust him. Why doona ye give me and Cooper a moment alone?"

Morna eyed him speculatively, one eyebrow raised astonishingly high as she relented. "Aye, I willna spell him if ye doona wish me to. 'Tis yer secret, I suppose."

Eoghanan waited until she'd shut the door behind her to shift toward Cooper. "Now, if we doona wish for Morna to take this knowledge from ye, ye must promise me that ye willna say a word to yer mother. Such a thing is difficult for most to understand. I doona think she would believe ye."

Cooper stuck his littlest finger up by Eoghanan's nose. "I promise, promise, promise. I won't say a word to anyone."

"What is that, lad?"

"It's a pinkie promise. Haven't you ever heard of those?"

Eoghanan shook, "No. What is it?"

"It...um...let me show you." The boy reached for his hand, bending in his thumb and folding his first three fingers over, leaving but the one smallest finger sticking out. "When we wrap our pinkies together it makes the promise stick."

It made no sense to him, but Eoghanan didn't question Cooper. "Aye, 'tis our secret then. Just ye and I."

Chapter 8

"What are you so smiley about?" I flipped the blanket and sheets back just far enough on the bed so that both Cooper and I could crawl in and, after climbing inside myself, patted the top of the bed for him to join me.

"I had the best day ever, Mom." Clad in his dinosaur pajamas, he climbed onto the bed but didn't slip beneath the covers, instead he sat on top of the comforter with his feet near my head so that he could face me.

"Ever? I didn't know you were such an enthusiastic fisherman, Coop." Placing both my hands behind my head, I settled in for a bit of conversation before sleep.

"I fish with Bebop all the time and I like it, but it wasn't the fishin'."

He had both hands extended back behind him to rest on and his feet swayed back and forth, happily.

"Well, what made it the 'best day ever,' then?"

"I can't tell you."

I rolled over on my side, smiling to the wall as I reached to turn off the lamp, "Oh, okay. Well, goodnight then, Coop. Love you."

Just as I put my finger on the lamp's knob, Cooper pounced on me. "No, Mom! Gimme a break. You know I wasn't through talking."

Laughing, I released my grip, rolling onto my back once more. "What is there to say if you won't tell me?"

He jumped from his current position and flipped himself over so that he lay on his stomach and rested his head on the palm of his hands. "It's not that I don't want to tell you. I can't. It's a secret."

Now he had my attention.

"Now, Coop, is this a secret someone told you, or one that

you learned by spying? Because those are two very different things, and we've already talked about this before—it's not okay to eavesdrop on people."

I watched him wrestle with my question, his face contorting as he lifted his brow and shifted his lower lip in between his teeth. As always, he didn't want to lie, but he knew I wouldn't like the truth either.

Instead, he rolled off the edge of the bed and silently walked over to my side, reaching up on his tip-toes to turn off the light. Enveloped in darkness, he crawled over me and onto the bed, slipping under the sheets on his side.

"I just got real sleepy, Mom. Goodnight. Angels on your pillow."

I rolled my eyes in the darkness, leaning over to kiss him on the forehead. "Angels on yours too, Coop. It was a little bit of both, huh?"

Silence followed my question for a minute or two, and then his voice, soft and sweet in its confession, answered.

"Yep, maybe a little."

* * *

I woke early, hoping to get a jump on looking through all the photographs I'd taken the day before and perhaps, get a little writing done on the article. Coop always rose early so it came as no surprise to find his half of the bed empty when I woke.

When he outgrew his crib several years ago, I moved him into his own room with a "big boy" bed. I made it my goal to figure out just what time he seemed to wake up each morning by setting my alarm at a different time each day—continually setting it earlier and earlier if I woke to find him already awake the day before. It didn't matter what time I set it, Coop's internal clock was determined to beat it. I would walk into his room every morning to find him playing with his toys. Eventually, I'd given up the effort and settled for rising by six each morning so that even if he woke earlier, he wouldn't be unsupervised for very long.

I knew he wouldn't have gone far and suspected he'd made his way downstairs to the kitchen, hoping to lend a helping hand with the breakfast preparations. Still, Cooper's idea of helping wasn't always viewed the same way by others. Deciding to forgo a shower for the moment, I brushed my hair and teeth, pulled on a pair of jeans and a t-shirt, and left in search of my son.

I heard him before I saw him, giggling at the deep Scottish voice making a gurgled, horrible sound that I could only assume was an attempt at a dinosaur noise.

Sure enough, as I descended the stairs, I saw Eoghanan sprawled out on his left side next to Cooper on the floor of the living room.

Each held a dinosaur—Cooper a small one with wings, Eoghanan a large t-rex. While Cooper had the advantage by keeping his dinosaur in the air, Eoghanan had his creature jumping to unimaginable heights for the short stubbiness of the dinosaur's legs. It sent Cooper into a fit of laughter each time.

"You're cheating." He said it smiling, not bothered by Eoghanan's imaginative dinosaur play. "That dinosaur couldn't jump like that."

"How do ye know that, lad? Have ye seen a dinosaur?"

By this point I'd reached the bottom of the stairs, but I stayed where they couldn't see me for a moment, not wishing to interrupt their conversation. Perhaps I knew where my son's penchant for eavesdropping came from, after all.

"No. Have *you*?" Cooper asked the question with such genuine curiosity that it left me baffled. Of course, Eoghanan had never seen a dinosaur, and Cooper knew it.

"No, lad. I havena traveled that far back. No at all."

For the life of me, I couldn't begin to imagine what they were talking about. Out of the loop and frustrated with my lack of understanding at their conversation, I decided to make my presence known.

"Good morning. Please tell me that you were awake when Coop found you." I looked sympathetically at Eoghanan as I neared, sitting down on the edge of the couch next to them.

"Aye, I was. I doona sleep verra much." Eoghanan shifted so that he could stand from his place on the floor, looking rather pleased with himself as he did so. "Ah, it feels nice to be able to move more freely. That dinna hurt me at all."

"Good, I'm so glad." I placed my hand on his back in a sort of congratulations. The warmth that shot through my fingers at the touch sent a jolt through my body. I enjoyed the unfamiliar feeling, but I felt him shiver a bit beneath my hand, and I jerked away awkwardly, worried that I'd made him uncomfortable. I had a tendency to be that way with people— to touch them in comfort or understanding. I supposed it was the mom in me.

Quickly, I bent to lift Cooper up into my arms to break the tension. After a good long hug, he pulled away, jerking his head toward the kitchen.

"Morna asked if I wanted to go work some sheep today."

I smiled at his statement, not sure if I was more pleased at how excited he seemed over some sheep or at prospect of having at least part of the day to look through my photos and write.

"Sheep, huh? Do you want to go?"

He thought my question ridiculous. I could tell from how his eyes bulged when I asked it, and he twisted free from my arms so that he could pull my hand back toward the staircase.

"Of course I want to go! I need to go put on some sheep working clothes, Mom. Let's go."

For being such a small kid, he did a fair job of pulling me across the floor. Shaking his hand free, I waved him ahead of me. "Go on, Coop. I'm right behind you."

Rubbing the sleepy from my eyes, I trudged up the stairs after him, watching as he stripped his pajama top even before reaching the bedroom door.

Chapter 9

I worked consistently throughout the morning, zoned into the screen of my laptop, clicking through photos and sporadically trying to get a start on the article, only deciding to take a break after the growl of my stomach became too loud to ignore.

As I made my way down the hallway, I created a mental task list, running through all of the places still left to explore and photograph, hoping I could remember them long enough to write them all down after grabbing a bite to eat. Midway down my mental list, as I passed the last door before the staircase, a deep scream inside Eoghanan's room made me shriek as I jumped as high as Cooper's t-rex.

"Grace?" Eoghanan's voice from somewhere inside the room calmed me immediately. I'd not realized that he'd stayed behind.

Cracked slightly, I stepped forward to push his bedroom door open, one hand on my rapidly beating heart in an attempt to slow it. I didn't find him in the main room, but I could hear him grumbling something from inside the bathroom and moved toward the sound of his voice.

"Eoghanan. Are you okay? Why did you scream?"

Unthinkingly, I stepped into the center of the room, giving me a direct view into the bathroom and a wide, gorgeous shot of Eoghanan's bare rear-end.

"Oh…gosh. So sorry." I jerked around quickly. My bare toe caught on the corner of the bed, sending me sprawling onto the floor, arms and legs spread wide.

Eoghanan laughed loudly. Although I kept myself on the floor, folding in one arm to shield my eyes, I could imagine his body shaking from the effort of it. As I listened to him step forward to help, I held up my other hand to stop him. "Wait.

Go get a towel or something."

With the only injured party being my big toe, I pushed myself up to stand and turned right into Eoghanan's approaching chest as he grabbed both my arms to steady me. With hesitation, I glanced downward and exhaled loudly in relief at finding him wrapped in a towel.

I didn't need to see him naked again. I'd not been on a date since before Cooper was born…or made for that matter, and the sight of that too perfect body left me quite hot and bothered.

"What was yer name again, lass? I doona think it can be Grace. 'Tis no verra fitting."

I laughed. He couldn't have been more right. "Yeah, it never has been very fitting. Why did you scream? And who showers with the door open?"

Reluctantly, I tore my gaze away from his chiseled chest and looked up to see his face contorting with embarrassment.

"I dinna expect ye to walk into me bedchamber, and I dinna scream. I doona scream, lass."

I rolled my eyes—typical man. "That was a scream if I've ever heard one."

"No," he released me, but reached up and thumbed my nose gently with his thumb and the corner of his forefinger. The gesture was playful, and I smiled as he moved back toward the bathroom. "Will ye help me with these beastly…," he hesitated, "ye call them knobs, aye?"

I nodded, my brows pulled in. He baffled me. How could a grown man, seemingly containing all his mental faculties, know so little?

I needn't say anything for him to see how odd I thought the question. "I told ye, lass. I dinna grow up amongst such things. I nearly melted me skin off trying to run the water."

"Alright." I stepped into the cramped bathroom with him, reaching down past him to fiddle with the shower knobs. "Just exactly where did you grow up? Did you wear a butt-flap and swing from the trees while being raised by monkeys?" He certainly had the physique to be a type of *Tarzan.*

Eoghanan shook his head, testing the water temperature with his fingers. "No, I doona think I've ever seen a monkey. Thank ye, the water feels much better."

He tugged at the corner of his towel, and I knew it was time to take my leave. That, or just jump right in with him. Appealing as the idea was, I thought it not the most ladylike of ideas.

"Good. I'll leave you to it then." I stopped walking just as he started to close the bathroom door, my own grumbling stomach reminding me of my manners. "Have you eaten anything in a while? I thought I'd go round up something for myself. I'll bring you up something, if you'd like."

I could just see his face in the doorway, and I couldn't help but think how likely it was that his towel had dropped already. "Aye, I'd love that, lass."

Smiling, he shut the door to me. Taking a breath to regain some sense of composure, I went down to the kitchen.

* * *

I spent the entire length of our salted cracker lunch apologizing at regular intervals for our lack of food choices. "You're going to be starving by dinner. I truly am sorry. It's as if she cooks her meals with magic. Seriously, I don't understand it. She's always cooking, but she has nothing in her cupboards. It's…" I truly had no word for it, "astonishing."

"Grace," he reached out and squeezed my hand, holding it long enough to quicken my pulse. "If ye apologize once more, I willna eat another bite. 'Tis no yer job, nor Morna's, to see me fed." Winking, he popped another cracker into his mouth.

I watched him eat, observing him closely. He lifted every cracker with his left hand, leaving his right arm hanging at his side. He did such a good job of compensating with his left arm that I'd not noticed how little he used his right. Still, something about the way he gripped things seemed a little unnatural, and I ventured a guess that he was actually right-handed. "You write with your right hand, don't you?"

The left corner of his mouth lifted and he shifted to face me. "Aye, and thankfully I still can do so, as long as I doona move me elbow too much. When the sword came down, it cut me deepest right along me shoulder muscle," he paused, lifting his left hand as he traced one of his fingers along the red line, showing me its path. "Then, it hit me bone and turned, traveling underneath and along me ribs. 'Tis made me right shoulder difficult to move, but Morna says it will heal eventually."

My eyes bugged nearly out of my head. Whatever I'd imagined as the cause of such an injury, I'd not considered a blade—a piece of machinery perhaps, but not a weapon. "A sword?"

"Aye, a mighty large one." He took a long look at my face, observing my look of shock. "Doona worry, lass. He's dead now—the man who did it."

He said it so dismissively that I couldn't help but swallow a laugh. He seemed to believe that I wondered more about whether the man who'd assaulted him was dead or alive, than why in hell someone had come at him with a sword in the first place.

Just as I opened my mouth to ask, he spoke again, changing the conversation entirely.

"I'm sorry if I frightened ye. Ye thought yerself alone, aye?"

"Yes, I did, but there's no need to apologize."

He nodded in acknowledgement of what I said and blew a long strand of unruly hair out of his face with his lower lip. He did it often, and I found myself wondering if months of being unable to lift his right shoulder had left him less groomed than he'd like.

"Would you…" I hesitated, hoping I wasn't about to

56

over-step. "Would you like me to cut it for you?" I pointed to the curly strand. "You sometimes act like it gets in your way, or I could at least pull it back?"

He glanced up, his eyes crossing as he made eye contact with the annoying strand. "If ye doona mind, but I wouldna wish to take ye from yer work."

"Ah," I waved a hand dismissively. "I'm done with that for now. This seems more urgent." I reached both hands up, slipping my fingers into his red locks, messing his hair around to get a feel for how it needed to be cut.

I'd cut Cooper's hair his whole life. Although their shade was different, the texture of their hair was very much the same—curly and, although not frizzy, the shiny curls on both men were not easily ruled, bouncing out of place at their whim. His neck relaxed as I played with his hair, and his eyes closed in pleasure. Men often didn't get to experience how lovely it felt to have their hair properly messed with.

"If ye insist, I doona have it in me to argue."

"I do. You'll feel much better when you get some of this off your neck." I stood and moved to stand behind him, lifting the hair at the base of his neck. He lay his head back in my hands, and I massaged his scalp as I gathered the strands. "Do you always keep your hair long?"

"Hmm…?"

His head relaxed so that I looked down at his face from above him, and he smiled as his eyes flickered open.

"What did ye ask me, lass? By God, that feels good, Grace."

"Yeah, a good head massage always does. I asked if you always keep your hair long."

"Oh, aye, but do what ye wish with it. I doona much care."

His eyes closed again, and I laughed, tugging on a strand at the base of his neck. "Hey, don't fall asleep on me. It'll be hard for me to cut your hair that way."

He reached his left hand up and grabbed my fingers, bringing them to rest in his hand and on his shoulder, "Oh, doona ye worry, I am verra, verra awake. 'Twould be impossible for me to sleep with yer hands on me."

I pulled away, pleased for the moment that his eyes were closed so he couldn't see my heated face. "Stand up and let's move your chair into the bathroom. I don't want to trim your hair over the carpet."

He did as I asked. Once he was vertical, I dragged his chair along onto the tile floor, surprised to find a pair of scissors resting in a small basket on the bathroom sink, along with wrapping cloths, washcloths, and a large jar of a homemade salve. "What's all this?" I asked as Eoghanan joined me, sitting down in the chair, immediately leaning his head back into my open hands.

"'Tis what Morna applies to me wound each day. Makes it herself."

"Up you go." I lifted his head and turned on the faucet, wetting my hands so that I could run them through his hair, re-wetting the strands so I could comb them through. "Have you been doctored today, yet?"

"No. I shall do it meself once ye have finished."

I examined his scar as I combed his hair. It would be a messy job if he tried to apply the salve himself, and I imagined it wouldn't feel good on his shoulder. "No. I'll do it when I'm finished."

"There's no need. The sight of me naked from a distance scared ye half to death. I doona wish to make ye see it more closely." He laughed a little, but there was a question in his statement.

With his head sufficiently wet and combed, I picked up the scissors and set to work, one curl at a time. "The only reason I turned away was because I'd not expected to find you naked, not because it hurt my eyes to look at you. Quite the opposite actually."

I couldn't hide the heat that spread up my neck this time, not with him staring up at me from the mirror. I'd truly meant to keep that last sentence inside my head and inwardly I grimaced. What was it about him that made me blurt things out without thinking?

I glanced up to see both corners of his mouth quirk a bit, trying to hold back a smile, but as soon as he caught my attention he let it loose. "Aye? Is that so, lass?" He twisted in his chair to look over his back at me.

Deciding there was no way to answer without embarrassing myself further, I placed my hands on either side of his head and twisted him back around to the front. "Unless you want to end up bald, I suggest you quit squirming in your seat."

He laughed loudly but obeyed, stiffening his shoulder as he sat up straight. "As ye wish, lass. As ye wish."

Chapter 10

Eoghanan woke the next morning energized in a way unfamiliar to him. Lying with his eyes still closed, he reveled in it—the newness of the feeling of a good night's sleep. Instead of waking on edge, his jaw clenched and shoulders tight, he woke to find a pleasant numbness radiating down his body. His shoulders loose, his mouth still wide from sound sleep. He usually never slept more than a few brief moments each night, waking often with his mind churning.

He'd not always been that way. As a young boy, still free and naïve of life's inevitable woes, he'd been able to sleep until the sun was far into the sky each day. The night of Osla's death, his brother Baodan's first wife, everything changed for him. Unable to save her, an impenetrable sense of failure and guilt settled over Eoghanan. Impenetrable, until now.

While the blade Niall had run down his body nearly killed him, it had also saved Eoghanan in ways he was just beginning to see. Without such an injury, he would never have journeyed to this strange time. He would never have met Grace.

Her presence here was no accident, of that he was now certain. Morna had lied to him before, when she'd said she didn't control where he went on his travels. She was too much of a matchmaker and the coincidence too strange to explain Grace's arrival at the small inn otherwise. The old witch had shown him the lass for a reason. Eoghanan couldn't help but hope it was to fulfill some missing piece of his soul.

For over seven years, he'd shut out any possibility of love for another woman, paying a silent penance for sins that weren't his own. Now that his brother knew the truth and his burden had been lifted, he was free to start his life anew. Free to become the man he'd once been, a man filled with passion, desire, and love. All of the things he'd denied himself for far too many years.

With his eyes still closed, he listened to Grace's voice near him and smiled. She stood outside his door, chattering so quickly he couldn't understand a word of what she said. He was content to simply listen to the rhythm of her voice.

Just thinking of her pushed away any remnants of sleepiness that remained. He couldn't remember the last time a lass stirred such a desire in him, and she desired him as well. Whether she intended to or not, she'd all but admitted as much to him.

Swinging his feet over the side of the bed to stand, he suddenly recognized the sound of his own name muttered amongst Grace's quickly spoken words. Moving silently across the floor, he pressed his ear against the door, anxious to hear what she said about him.

"What?"

Grace's voice sounded shocked. He waited for whomever she spoke with to repeat their question. When none did, he realized she spoke to the telephone—an odd contraption Morna had spent the better half of an hour trying to explain to him with little success. He couldn't understand the need to reach someone so immediately, unless to bring news of a death or threat thereof. Still, he pressed his ear closer, hoping to learn enough from Grace's side of the conversation to gain its meaning.

* * *

"What?" I laughed, more from shock than my thinking her funny. It couldn't have been a serious question.

"You heard what I said. I asked if you'd let him bury the bone yet?" My sister snorted as she asked the question a second time, pleased at her own juvenile wittiness.

"Ok, first of all, of course I haven't. And second of all, eww. Please don't refer to sex that way ever again, Jane."

"Goodness, it is so easy to get a rise out of you, Grace."

Jane laughed loudly into the phone, and I could imagine her delighted smile.

"All I said was that there was someone else staying at the inn with me and Cooper. He..." I stuttered. It only made sense that Jane would come to the conclusion that something was going on between Eoghanan and me. Why else would I bring him up? It's not as if it was unusual for operating inns to have more than one guest at a time. I'd simply found myself wanting to talk about him, to discuss him with someone who wasn't five years old. "He seems very nice is all. Cooper really likes him."

"Hmm..." Jane waited a moment, presumably hoping I would say more. When I didn't, she continued. "Cooper, likes him huh? It isn't Grace that likes him? Are you telling me that not even a small part of you wants to see him naked?"

I smiled, unable to repress a grin at the memory of him standing gloriously nude in his bathroom. "I didn't say that. Maybe it's not *just* Cooper that likes him. And actually, I've already seen him naked."

The guffaw-ey gasp that came from the other end of the phone made me immediately regret the admission.

"What? I thought you said you hadn't slept with him."

A sudden thump against Eoghanan's door caused me to murmur a quick, "Hang on just a sec," before throwing the phone down next to its base. I cautiously rested an ear against Eoghanan's door, listening for any movement. Obviously, he still slept. If he'd been up, I knew there was a chance he could have heard me. I was literally half a foot away from his door. Breathing a sigh of relief, I stepped away, picking up the receiver once more to continue my explanation. "I didn't sleep with him. I walked in on him about to take a shower. Jerked away so fast, I tripped over the edge of his bed."

More laughter. "So...what did he look like? Good, I'm guessing since you flipped out."

As ridiculous as it was, my knees became a bit watery at

the memory. "A-m-a-zing." My sisters were the only people who could get me to revert from the full-grown mother I was today to the boy-crazed teenage girl I had once been. Of all my sisters, Jane was especially talented at this.

"Well then, get you some of that action. That would be such a great story to carry back with you when you come home." She changed her voice in a very poor attempt to mimic my own. "You see, I was going to marry Jeffrey, my very best friend in the whole world, but then I came to my senses and fled the wedding. I flew to Scotland the very next day for work. While I was there, I had a wild fling with a native Scot." She dropped the mimic, back to being Jane. "I'm serious, that's an awesome story. One to tell your grandkids one day."

I ran a hand through my hair in exasperation. "No grandkid ever wants to hear about their grandmother's wild fling, Jane. Ever." Glancing at my watch, I decided it best that I direct the conversation to the whole reason I called so I could get back to work. "Besides, we seem to have gotten very side-tracked here. I just wanted to check in on Mom and Father. On a scale of one-to-ten, just how angry is he?"

She paused—evidently it was a ten. "I don't know. Maybe…maybe like an 8.75."

It was a very 'Jane' answer. "8.75?"

"Yeah. I mean, he really didn't get as angry as I expected, but once we noticed you were gone, I expected that he'd literally turn into some sort of dragon and just burn the hell out of everybody. He didn't. He's still human, so yeah, less angry than I expected. He's still very, very pissed though. It was weird, like a small part of him expected it. That being said, I cannot imagine the earful Jeffrey got from him. Not the best of times to leave him to deal with Father, although I know you had to for work."

"I know, I know." I'd been trying my best not to think of what I'd left Jeffrey with. It made my gut twist with guilt. "I really need to get back to work. I just wanted to check in on things. I love you, Jane."

"I love you too, Grace." I could envision her leaning her head tenderly into the ear piece, just as she would have done to my shoulder had I been standing next to her. "I'm proud of you, ya know? We all are. Mom, me, everyone except Father, I imagine. The whole thing was ridiculous. I'm glad you didn't go through with it."

"Me too." I couldn't express just how glad I was. For the first time in my entire life, I felt like I'd truly liberated myself from my father's ruling thumb. "Talk soon." I hung up the phone, determined to get at least a little work done.

* * *

His cheeks hurt from grinning, not accustomed to staying in the lifted position at such length. Though, try as he might, Eoghanan couldn't relax his smile. Once Grace had ended her telephone conversation, he slumped against the wall in relief. There'd been a brief moment where she almost found him, with both their ears pressed against his doorway while he held his breath in the hopes that she wouldn't hear him.

Although he could only hear one side of the conversation, Grace had only said good things about him. Wonderful things. She'd said that she liked him, and that Cooper did also. Eoghanan couldn't be more pleased to hear it. He very much liked the wee lad, and he liked the boy's mother even more.

She'd also spoken about his naked body. While he was not familiar with the word she'd used to describe it, the tone of her voice held no note of displeasure. Rather, she'd said it breathlessly, and his linen breeches had grown tight instantly. Only one thing gave him pause—the absence of Cooper's father. He assumed the man was dead, but there was no way to be certain.

Rested and fully alive, Eoghanan peeked outside into the hallway. Finding it empty, he went in search of Jerry. He wished to ask the lass to do something special, but he needed advice on what the times called for and to find assurance that Grace was free to be pursued.

He found Jerry in the back, tending the inn's small garden with Morna.

"Ach, there ye are, lad. Morna and I have something to ask ye."

Eoghanan lifted a brow in surprise, nodding in encouragement that they continue.

Morna stepped toward him, placing her hand on the side of his arm. "Jerry and I made a dinner reservation in the city a while back, but I doona think either one of us is up to it this evening. We thought perhaps ye might like to take Grace in our place."

"Reservation?"

"Aye, at a lovely place in the center of Edinburgh. I have directions, and I have something fitting for ye to wear. Why doona ye ask her? She'll say yes, I know it. Be sure to tell her that she will have to drive, though. Tell her that ye canna due to yer injured shoulder. She willna mind."

The witch could obviously read his mind for she presented him with the very opportunity he wished before he asked for it—a special evening alone with Grace.

With all his excitement, he forgot the other question he meant to ask as he walked away.

Chapter 11

Eoghanan's invitation came as a surprise, albeit a lovely one. Or, perhaps it really wasn't too much of a surprise when I thought back on all the subtle flirtation of the previous day. Still, it had been so long since I'd been asked out on any sort of date, I'd begun to believe that my last first date over six years ago would be my last date ever.

He asked in the most adorable way. Knocking on the door of my bedroom and speaking to Cooper first, saying something along the lines of, "I believe Morna needs yer assistance, young Cooper. Seems that she's found a snail in an unfortunate place and doesna wish to pick it up herself."

Cooper, eager to help and overly excited by anything remotely gross, leapt up from his place on the floor. "A snail? Well, I'll get it for her."

Cooper ran down the stairs quickly, leaving Eoghanan and I alone, where he shifted back and forth nervously in my doorway for a minute before speaking.

"Grace, do ye have a dress with ye here?"

I turned my head inquisitively, smiling internally at his question. It seemed an odd way to start the conversation. "Uh, yeah I do actually. It's not all-together fancy, more of just a sundress. Why do you ask?"

"I hoped that ye might join for me dinner in Edinburgh. Would ye like to? I should tell ye that ye will have to steer the car. I doona think me shoulder will allow it."

"Edinburgh?" I couldn't help the surprise and hesitation in my voice. It wasn't like Edinburgh was just down the road. "That's over three hours away."

"Ah." He looked down at his feet a bit, embarrassed. "So, no then? 'Tis no the best idea."

"No." I moved toward him, shaking my head to stop him.

"That's not what I said. I'm only a bit surprised is all."

"Aye."

I smiled, hoping my initial reaction hadn't disappointed him. A drive that far would get the both of us out of the inn for an entire day, which appealed to me greatly. I imagined he was in dire need of it as well. I doubted he'd traveled outside a ten-mile radius of the inn since arriving there. In addition, it might also be good for work, if I could stop and take some photos along the way. "I think that sounds great. I can be ready in half an hour." I glanced over at the mirror on the wall across from me and looked sheepishly back at him. "Forty-five tops. What about Cooper?"

"If 'tis alright with ye, Morna said that she and Jerry might take him to explore Conall Castle. 'Tis just down the road a ways."

Cooper would be thrilled at the idea. "He'll love that. Meet you downstairs in a bit?"

He smiled, nodded once, and left me alone to get ready. I started stripping my clothes as soon as the door closed, resigning myself to the fact that, once again, I would get little work done today. It was becoming a very bad habit.

* * *

"Are ye certain I doona look a fool? Do men no wear kilts in Scotland anymore?" Eoghanan looked down at the khaki slacks and dark blue shirt Morna had dressed him in feeling utterly unsure about his new outfit. The linen pants and stretchy shorts were sensible garb for lounging around the inn, for they kept pressure off his scar, but to appear in front of other people without his kilt seemed very strange to him.

"Ye look nothing like a fool. Ye look like a man every lass in the Highlands will want to jump on sight. Best keep Grace on yer arm so they know ye are taken."

"Taken?" It seemed a fast conclusion for the old lass to come to, though he liked the way it sounded very much. "I barely know the lass. Taken is no the right word."

Eoghanan watched as Morna clucked her tongue at him, dismissively.

"If ye say so, though I doona know why ye would doubt a thing I say to ye. I have me way of knowing things that others do not."

He knew that better than anyone, but said nothing as he heard Grace's footsteps on the stairs, turning to take the sight of her in as she approached him. She was a beautiful lass by any standard. Even casually dressed as she'd been every time he'd seen her in the strange pants that women wore in this time with her long hair pulled up loosely off her neck and out of her eyes, he thought her breathtaking.

But now, dressed in a light blue dress that reached just past her knees, the sleeves capping just over her shoulders, he could scarcely catch his breath. She'd let her hair down. The long blonde strands fell loosely about her shoulders, trailing down her neck and into the deep crevice between her breasts that were emphasized by the cut of the fabric.

Suddenly Morna's hand smacked him roughly against the back, reminding him to look up from the lush paleness of her bosom and to speak up like a grown man rather than the young lad he suddenly felt like.

"Grace. That is…well…a verra nice dress."

He smiled as she laughed, some of his nervousness lifting away as she tucked her hand gently into the crook of his arm. "Thanks, you don't look bad yourself. Nice haircut."

"Aye." He grinned lifting his left hand to touch a small spot on the back of his head, winking at her as he did so. "Only exception being this wee bit here. The lass who trimmed it got rather excited for a moment."

Cooper suddenly spoke next to Grace's side, and Eoghanan realized rather ashamedly that he'd not noticed the boy trailing along behind her before. "That's so weird. What did you do? Tickle her? She's never messed up my hair."

Grace glanced up at him a little sheepishly, and he reached down to grip Cooper on the shoulder. "Aye, yer mother did a fine job. I only spoke in jest. Are ye excited about yer trip with Morna and Jerry?"

"Oh yes. So, so, so excited. I've never seen a real castle before. Only on tv and stuff."

Grace stepped away from him, bending over to pick up Cooper and hug him. "I'm sure you're going to have a great time. Just promise me that you'll listen to whatever they say, Coop?"

The young lad regarded her seriously. "Of course I will, Mom. I only get rowdy for you, ya know?"

Grace laughed, leaning in to kiss Cooper's forehead. "Yes, I do know. Thanks for that."

The boy laughed, squirming so she would set him down. "You're welcome."

Once Cooper retreated toward Morna and Jerry, Grace looped her arm around Eoghanan once more, sending his pulse racing in anticipation of their day spent together. "Let's get out of here," she whispered in his ear. Gladly, he turned her toward the door.

* * *

For the first half hour of our drive, Eoghanan remained unusually silent. If I'd not been watching him closely out of the corner of my eye, I would've worried that he'd been less interested than he'd first appeared. Instead, I found that it wasn't a lack of interest in conversation with me, but a rather obvious fascination with the workings of the car that kept him silent.

He watched everything I did closely; from adjusting the mirrors to shifting the gears, he watched with wide eyes, and his mouth kept opening and closing in the same way Cooper's often did if he wished to ask a question but then thought better of it. And although it appeared as if he tried to hide it, I sensed an unexplainable nervousness about him as I pushed the car to a reasonable cruising speed.

"Do cars make you nervous?"

Eoghanan directed his attention fully to me for the first time since the beginning of the car ride and smiled, shaking his head in a fashion that seemed more about pushing away his thoughts than in answer to my question. "No, though ye do."

"Me?" The thought that I made him nervous seemed entirely absurd to me, but the confession endeared me to him even more. He had the unique ability to seem completely confident, yet vulnerable, at the same time.

"Aye. Ye are stunning, Grace. I have never seen anyone as beautiful as ye and it...aye, I canna help but be nervous around ye. 'Tis a verra nice feeling."

"You like to be nervous?" As a mother, I lived in a constant state of light anxiety. I disliked nothing more than being nervous.

"Aye."

He reached over, laying his hand on my knee—a gesture that sent a shockwave so great down my spine I had to grip the wheel to keep from swerving off the road.

"Nerves, as ye call them, remind me that I can feel something other than regret and worry. I havena felt that way about much of anything in a verra long time."

"Oh." I hardly knew what to say in response to him. It pained me to think that he'd lived with such feelings, but he also meant to tell me that I made him feel differently, which was the headiest of compliments.

My entire body hummed with an unexplainable energy anytime I was near him, but in the confines of the car it seemed worse, like the windows would vibrate and shatter if some of the pressure wasn't released soon.

Glancing out the side window, I spotted a hill scattered with flowers that truthfully, while pretty enough was rather ordinary. I pulled the car over all the same, desperate to put some space between us before I jumped him.

Eyeballs deep in mommy-world since Cooper's birth, I'd gone far too long without the affection of a man. In Eoghanan's presence, a gentleman if I'd ever seen one, someone who I knew couldn't tell a lie by the look in his eyes, a man who actually seemed to like me as much as I did him, well, it was like that part of me, the part of me who wanted to be kissed and touched and loved by a man had been suddenly unleashed after years of captivity.

And I was very, very hungry.

Chapter 12

Eoghanan must have felt the same building pressure and the need to get a grip on it before continuing the rest of the journey into Edinburgh as I had, for when we returned to the car after my abrupt stop, he made a pointed effort to engage in conversation the rest of the way. At least while we listened and responded to one another, our minds weren't left to daydream about ripping each other's clothes off. Not that he would've acted on it anyway. He came across as far too old-fashioned to do so.

We even managed to keep the conversation going throughout dinner, though it consisted of mainly pointless jabber. We discussed my work a lot, Scotland, the inn, Morna and Jerry, but nothing overly personal. It was as if there lay some unspoken understanding between us that anything personal that might evoke emotion would put us in that place again—the state of desire that would build the tension that lay ever present between us, and it frightened us both. Though he'd said nothing of the sort, and it seemed hard to believe by looking at him, I got the feeling that perhaps he was just as 'out of the game' as I was. Just as unfamiliar with what was expected on a date, just as silently eager for a human connection.

When we'd finished eating and our bill paid, a strained silence fell over us once again, but this time I made no effort to end it, exhausted from hours of forced conversation. I couldn't help but be a little disappointed, only because I knew this date wasn't a fair representation of how we could be together. Though we'd not spoken too much, we'd only known each other a few days after all, conversation flowed more naturally with him than with anyone I had ever met before. He scared me, or more accurately, the way he made me feel scared me, and I'd allowed my fear to dictate our conversation. I expected he'd done the same, and we rode most of the way back to the inn mutually, but silently, feeling like we'd let the other, not to mention ourselves, down.

Finally, less than a mile away from the inn, Eoghanan spoke, reaching over to squeeze my hand as he did so. "That was rotten, lass. I doona wish to discuss the weather, nor the countryside with ye. 'Tis no why I asked ye to come here, no to speak to ye as I would a stranger. I know that I havena known ye but a few days, but it doesna feel that way. No to me. I doona believe it does to ye either. I wish to know everything about ye, about what ye did as a child, about yer family. I want ye to tell me what ye want out of yer life and for wee Cooper's, and I wish to tell ye about meself as well. I want to speak to ye about things that matter, but I canna do that just yet."

"Why not?" It was the only thing I could force myself to say in response to him. He gave the perfect speech—exactly what every woman wants to hear—that a man wanted to actually learn more about you…by means of communication. Something that every man I'd ever known until now found very challenging.

I don't think I would've believed such an exclamation from just anyone, but I knew that he told the truth. He was different; I could tell that from the first moment I saw him. He didn't play games, didn't pretend to be someone he wasn't.

It took him a moment to answer. I could sense his hesitation in the way he gripped my hand. He kept squeezing it, releasing it, squeezing it again, all the while running his thumb back and forth over the top of my hand.

"Because…" he exhaled loudly, and I slipped my thumb from underneath his hand, bringing it around to stroke his hand to comfort him. My mommy-gene, my inherent need to soothe, coming through once again.

"Lass, if ye told me those things just now, all of the

important details about ye, I wouldna hear them. I can think of nothing other than what yer hair would feel like if I ran my fingers through it, how yer lips would feel against me own. So please, continue to speak to me about the weather and yer boss, Mr. Perdie, but remember that I do wish to hear everything else. I just canna hear it right now. No when I'm so bewitched by ye."

I replayed his words in my head over and over. Each time they sounded more swoon-worthy than the last. My heart beat in quick time, and I had to hold my breath because I knew it would come out shaky. I said nothing, only slowly pressed down on the brake and pulled the car to the side of the road.

He mistook my response. As I threw the car into park and unbuckled my seatbelt, he started to apologize. "Ach, I've behaved as a fool, Grace. Forgive me. I dinna mean any disrespect to ye. I meant it as a compliment. I dinna wish for ye to think that I was bored with ye. I know the conversation may have seemed that way. I'm sorry. Truly. I doona know…I am no verra good at speaking with women."

"Hush." I was certain my eyes were hazy with lust. I scarcely knew how to handle the emotion, it had been so very long since I'd felt it. My entire body trembling with my desire for him, I placed one finger on his lips, just long enough to silence him and then I pressed my lips against his.

It surprised him, I could tell by his short intake of breath, but he responded immediately. Groaning into my mouth, a deep, guttural noise that made my stomach muscles clench as his left hand moved to the back of my head, pulling me closer.

It was perfect, yet restrictive. I couldn't stand to continue kissing him with the barrier of the console between us. I wanted him closer, wanted to deepen our kiss. "Wait. I…" my words were shaky. I breathed deeply trying to catch my breath. "I did that too soon. I'm sorry."

He laughed a bit, but allowed me to pull away. "It was no too soon for me, lass."

"That's not what I meant." I started the car, throwing it into drive so that we could get back to the inn and resume our kissing outside the vehicle. "I want to be closer to you than I can be in the car. Let me get us to the inn."

I saw his grin from the corner of my eye as he moved to brush a strand of hair behind my ear. "Do ye? Well, I willna deny ye that."

I couldn't finish the remaining mile fast enough, but after seeing lights still on inside the inn, I parked the car quietly, hoping Cooper wouldn't see us pull up. He'd rush outside to greet us if he did.

We exited the car in sync and, after a brief moment, I crushed myself against him once again, not hearing the front door of the inn open or the footsteps that approached us as I lost myself in Eoghanan's kiss.

"Mom, look who's here."

I stilled instantly, mortified that my young son had caught me making out like some hormone-crazed teenager. I didn't even care who was there, nothing or no one could embarrass me more than I already was...or so I thought.

"Tough day of work, huh Grace?" Jeffrey stood next to Cooper, smiling with shocked eyes.

Then Cooper's voice, all high and pitchy with excitement, "it's Dad!"

Chapter 13

"Jeffrey!" My voice was perilously close to matching Cooper's pitch and, although there was no reason for me to feel this way, guilt swarmed over me. I'd been doing nothing wrong, but seeing Eoghanan's horrified expression made me feel like I had.

"Da?" Eoghanan took a huge step away from me, putting a wide gap between us. He glanced back and forth between me and Cooper and Jeffrey, his brows turning in deeper with each flick of his eyes. "I think I'll retire, Grace."

His voice was hard as he walked away. While I wished to go after him, there were other people I had to deal with first. I waited until the inn door closed behind Eoghanan then I stepped forward to hug Cooper and then Jeffrey.

"What are you doing here?"

"I decided it wasn't worth it to stay and listen to your father. I turned over my clients to other lawyers and decided to join the two of you." Jeffrey winked down at Cooper who was ecstatic at how Mom's business trip had turned into a family vacation for him.

"Oh." I knew Jeffrey could see the disappointment on my face, and I rushed to clarify. "It's not that I'm displeased to see you. You'll be a big help if you'll keep Cooper occupied while I work. It's just…" I jerked my head back to the car to indicate what they'd walked up on. "I just wish you'd waited a minute to make your appearance."

Jeffrey pulled the corner of his lip down in apology. "Yeah, sorry about that. The way Cooper talked about it, I just didn't put it together that it was that sort of dinner. Guess you better go after him to do some explaining, huh?"

Before I could answer, he bent to pick up Cooper, "You ready to go to bed?" Cooper yawned and laid his head on his dad's shoulder. His excitement had worn him flat out. Jeffrey turned his attention back to me. "Go, Grace. We can talk more in the morning. The old lady, Morna, right? Anyhow, she put me in my own room. I'll take Cooper with me."

"Ok, thank you." I kissed Jeffrey on the cheek and Cooper on the top of his head, holding open the door for Jeffrey so he could carry Cooper through it.

"Hey, Grace." He paused at the base of the stairs, looking at me over his shoulder. "Good on you. It's good to see you smile—get out a bit. It's time."

*   *   *

He didn't answer on my first knock so I hollered at him as I rapped my knuckles against the door a second time.

"Eoghanan. Look, I know all that didn't make me look so good. Will you open the door so I can explain?"

The handle turned slowly to reveal a stone-faced Eoghanan. He stood blocking the doorway. Clearly, I wouldn't be permitted inside.

"I am angry with ye, Grace. I doona think there is need for explanation. 'Twas verra apparent."

"No, believe me, there's a great need for explanation. It's a complicated situation."

He made a noise that lay somewhere between a groan and a laugh. A noise that gave away just how truly hurt and angry he was. "I doona doubt that lass, but I doona wish to hear it. Goodnight."

He shut the door.

The breeze that followed froze my face.

Chapter 14

"Good morning." I entered Jeffrey and Cooper's room bearing coffee and orange juice. Although I didn't much feel like it, I couldn't help but smile at the sight of Cooper and his dad coloring together.

Jeffrey stood as I entered, reaching desperately for his coffee. "You're amazing. Thank you. Last night didn't go so well, huh?"

"Why do you say that?" Setting Cooper's orange juice down on the floor next to him, I started in on my own cup of coffee.

"Give me some credit, Grace. I know you. I know that," he pointed to my forehead, "the large vein that runs across the top of your head bulges with you're stressed or upset. It's bulging big time this morning."

"Great." I rubbed at the vein and then stopped, knowing it would only aggravate it more. "You're right though. He wasn't in the mood to let me explain. I don't know if he'll ever be." Waving a hand dismissively, I took a large gulp of coffee. "Just as well, I guess. It would be a bad idea to get involved. Ya know, since he lives in Scotland and we live in New York."

"What a load of crap, Grace."

He was absolutely right, but if I admitted that, I knew I'd get all sad and mopey. I had too much work to do for that.

"No, it's not. It's practical. This is a work trip, and that's what I plan on doing today. Coop and I are going to be gone taking photos this afternoon. Want to join us?"

"No. I think I'll hang around here." There was an expression on his face that made me nervous. An expression that said, 'I have definite plans, but I'd just rather you didn't know about them'.

"Are you sure? What is there for you to do around here?

You're not planning on saying anything to Eoghanan are you? Because there's no point. Please don't."

"Yeah, I'm sure. I plan on sleeping most of the day, not meddling in your dating life."

Dating life. He said it like I usually had one. I didn't think that one date could be considered equivalent to my having a dating life—dating incident, perhaps. "Sleep is the worst thing you could do for your jet lag. You'll never get adjusted that way."

He rolled his eyes. "I'm adjusted. I'm just exhausted and want to spend a lazy day doing nothing but sleeping and eating."

"Okay, fine. Just don't say anything to him, okay?"

"Sure thing, Grace. Sure thing."

*　*　*

Eoghanan slept fitfully, visions of Grace's face as her husband walked up on them kissing, floating up behind his eyelids each time he tried to shut his eyes. He thought over the events of the previous evening repeatedly, each time all of it making less sense than the last.

He'd seen it on her face, the guilt, the regret she felt at kissing him. She'd not been pleased to be seen with him. It had been his mistake really, to assume Cooper's father was dead. He didn't understand enough of the customs of today's times to have another explanation for why the lass and her son would have traveled such a great distance alone.

How ironic that he would be accused of having an affair once when he was innocent only to be guilty in a different one without his knowledge. It was unfair of Grace to treat him thus, to pull him into such a situation. Surely, he'd not behaved in such a way to make her think he was the kind of man who would kiss another man's wife.

One aspect of the evening confused him more than any other. Why had the man Grace had called Jeffrey not knocked him on his arse for placing such intimate hands on his wife? He certainly would have had it been him. Instead, the man had smiled at them both, with no show of anger in his eyes.

As if summoned by mere thought, Eoghanan opened his door to the rough knocking of the very man he'd been thinking about.

The man held the same unsettling smile. Surely it wasn't a common thing for men to share their women so leisurely in this time. The man extended his hand toward him. Ignoring the painful pull of his shoulder, Eoghanan met the man's hand with his own.

"Uh, hello. I didn't get to properly introduce myself last night. Name's Jeffrey. Do you mind if I talk to you a minute?"

"I'm Eoghanan. Aye, come in." Eoghanan stepped aside to allow the man entry, wondering if now would be when the man might swing a fist in his direction. Perhaps he'd only refrained from doing so last night so that young Cooper wouldn't see the altercation.

"Listen." Jeffrey faced him just as soon as he'd stepped inside. "I need to talk to you about Grace."

Of course, why else would this stranger need to speak with him? "Aye, I believe I owe ye an apology. I willna lay the blame on Grace, but I dinna know that ye were married. I wouldna have…I wouldna have kissed her if I had."

"What? Grace and I are not married. I'm not the one you need to apologize to, not at all. As long as you don't hurt her, you go ahead and kiss Grace all you want to. I imagine it would do her some good."

Jeffrey clasped him on his injured shoulder, and Eoghanan had to clamp down on his teeth to keep from groaning with pain. His head hurt. He'd not felt such an overwhelming lack of understanding in a very long time.

"So ye are no Grace's husband, but ye are Cooper's father? Forgive me, I doona think I understand the situation."

Jeffrey shrugged and started to make his way back to the

doorway. "Yes, I'm Cooper's father, but not Grace's husband. It's a weird situation. Look, I already told Grace I wouldn't say anything to you, so I'm not going to say anything else. I just wanted you to know that whatever conclusion you jumped to last night is undoubtedly wrong. Talk to her." Eoghanan nodded, unsure of what else to say. Nodding in return, Jeffrey turned his back to him, retreating two steps toward the doorway before twisting to speak to him once more.

"Oh, and one other thing. Grace may not be my wife, but she's my family. I have a strong feeling that you made her cry last night. I didn't see her do it, but this morning her head was all veiny and her eyes all red. That is not okay. You make her cry ever again, and I'll knock you flat on your ass. I don't care if you're eight inches taller than me. Got it?"

Eoghanan repressed a grin. Stranger or no, anyone who would rise to Grace's defense in such a manner had his respect and admiration. "Aye."

"Good. Well then, have a good day. See ya around."

Jeffrey turned and left, leaving Eoghanan smiling in the doorway. He'd gather more explanation from Grace later. He'd already heard the most important part—the lass wasn't married and so his own hope could remain.

Chapter 15

After I'd spoken with Jeffrey, I spent the rest of the day working. I drove down the road to Conall Castle, allowing Cooper to show me the best places to take pictures after he'd told me he'd looked around especially for them during his trip there with Jerry and Morna. While not the first places I would have chosen to photograph, it thrilled me that my son was so thoughtful. I gladly followed him around, letting him lead for the day.

By the time we returned to the inn, Coop was more than ready to spend some time with his dad, which gave me the evening to work on the article. I worked steadily, determined to keep my mind off of Eoghanan and my frustration at him for not allowing me to explain myself. As much as I wanted to hash things out, I'd spent too much of my childhood around a man who wouldn't listen to what I had to say whenever I needed him to hear me the most. Though, I didn't believe this was a common character trait of Eoghanan, his refusal to listen made me feel like the repressed child, teenager, and then young mom that I'd once been. I was through trying to reason with someone who didn't want to hear it.

Jeffrey knocked on every door, every time he did so, in just the same way—three knocks, brief silence, followed by three more knocks. Cooper never knocked and neither did Morna or Jerry, so as soon as I heard a knock on my door, I knew who it was. Part of me had known that Jeffrey wouldn't keep his promise. Subconsciously, I think that's why I asked it of him. I didn't want him to.

Taking a breath, I stood, closed my laptop, and readied myself to give Eoghanan a full explanation, not that I believed it would make any real difference, no matter how much I wanted it to. Still, I couldn't bear the thought of Eoghanan believing me a liar or a cheat. My little family—Jeffrey, Cooper, and me—was unusual and difficult for anyone outside it to really understand. It was part of the reason I'd avoided the dating scene since Cooper's birth. I didn't want to have to explain how it worked, to promise over and over that nothing was going on between Jeffrey and me, that nothing ever had.

"Grace, I need to speak to ye if ye will allow it, lass."

"Of course I will," I answered him as I swung the door open, stepping aside so that he would enter. I closed the door behind him, and to my surprise, turned right into his arms.

He hugged me tightly, apologizing with his chin against the top of my head. "I am no a good man, Grace. I dinna know what to think when wee Cooper and Jeffrey walked up on us, but I should have allowed ye to explain. 'Tis only that I'd no felt as happy as I did when I held ye in me arms for ages. When I saw them, believing that ye'd lied to me…it hurt me more deeply than I'd like to admit. I dinna behave as I should have."

I rubbed his back gently with my hand, speaking against his chest. "I'm sorry, too. It just seemed a bit early to explain everything, and I never thought Jeffrey would show up here. He talked to you, I guess?"

He nodded, and his chin felt much more boney against my head than it truly was.

"What did he tell you?"

I couldn't see Jeffrey getting into too deep of an explanation. While he spoke to me about everything, he wasn't that way with most people. I imagined he would have told Eoghanan only what was necessary to convince him to let me explain.

Eoghanan released me and paced around the room a bit, confirming what I'd already guessed. Jeffrey had told him little. Eoghanan still appeared quite confused by the entire situation.

"No verra much. He said that 'twas yer story to tell, and

he's right. I should have allowed ye to do so. All Jeffrey told me was that ye are no married to him, which is what I thought when Cooper called him Da."

"Well…" I moved to sit on the end of my bed, patting the mattress so that he would join me. Before last night, I would have worried about Cooper walking in and seeing a man in his mother's room but, now that his father was here, Coop had gleefully moved into his dad's bedroom to spend his nights there. "I almost was. Just last week, actually."

"Ah." I watched as Eoghanan's body tensed slightly, but he still moved to sit next to me. "So ye are no married to him, but ye are his?"

Placing Jeffrey inside any sort of context where I belonged to him made me squirm internally. I shook my head, reaching for both of Eoghanan's hands. "No. If you don't hear anything else I say, hear that. Jeffrey and I are not an item and we *never* have been."

His thick brows pulled in tight. He was trying to see, to understand what I meant, but understandably, he was having trouble. "But ye have a child together?"

"Yes, but we didn't…Jeffrey isn't Cooper's real father." I looked down at our hands, mine squeezing his tightly, his thumb moving back and forth as he'd done last night.

He exhaled loudly, as if he'd been holding his breath for a long time. We sat there, each of us avoiding the other's gaze, our heart rates slowly escalating, the tension between us building once again.

Eventually, he pulled one of his hands away, moving it to my chin as he lifted my face to make me look at him. "I still doona think I understand all there is to know, but ye are saying that ye and Jeffrey are no married and willna ever be. That ye are no spoken for by anyone else, aye?"

I couldn't help but smile. 'Spoken for?' It seemed archaic language. Why didn't he just say, 'Are you dating anyone else?' Regardless, Eoghanan said many things in such a way, and he made it sound charming every time. "Yes, that is what I'm saying." I held eye contact, determined not to break it so that he would understand that point. "I am entirely single."

"I am pleased to hear it, lass."

"Do you want to hear the rest?" I pulled away a bit so that I could kick off my shoes, standing so that I could pull my legs beneath me, settling into a more comfortable position.

"Aye. Verra much so."

"Okay. Settle in."

And so I began. I told him about my father's job, the old money that he came from, not to mention the mounds of money he made on his own, all of it combining to create our family's New York estate. How I'd grown up around unimaginable, disgusting wealth and that Jeffrey, along with his father, had been the primary grounding force throughout my entire life.

"I met Jeffrey when I was four. My father hired both his parents, his mother to work as a maid in our household and his father to manage our grounds. The family moved into one of the small cottages on our estate and, since Jeffrey and I were the same age, we just took to each other." I paused, checking out Eoghanan, to see if he grew bored. It wasn't the shortest of stories. He couldn't have appeared more attentive.

He patted my hand gently. "Go on, lass. I wish to hear everything."

So I continued. "I fell in love with Jeffrey and his family, spending more time in their cottage than our mansion because I felt wanted there. I was close to my sisters, and to a lesser degree, my mom, but we were a house divided. All of us girls versus my dad. It made for a cold, stressed, disingenuous environment.

"Jeffrey's family did everything under a canopy of the love they felt for one another and it was contagious. Jeffrey's mother died when we were eight, and it was the most devastating event of my childhood. I remember thinking that I was more heartbroken at her death than I would have been at my own father's because I knew that Maggie loved me. To this day, I don't know that about my father."

I swallowed the lump that rose in my throat.

"Anyway, Jeffrey and I leaned on each other a lot during that time. He became my brother, my best friend, and we've just always stayed like that. In college, I started dating this guy, an exchange student from Australia. He was a real loser, and deep down I knew that. But after years of trying to be perfect, I wanted something wild, fun. The Aussie definitely was that. Jeffrey couldn't stand him, but he did end up giving me the one thing I care most about in the entire world— Cooper."

I sighed, the memory never a pleasant one.

"When I told him I was pregnant, he bounced, as in, he actually left and flew back home to Australia. I never heard from him after that. Jeffrey stepped in even before I told my family. And now..." I was ready to finish my explanation. Talking about myself wasn't my favorite thing to do by any stretch of the imagination. "Jeffrey is Cooper's dad in every way that matters. But, Jeffrey and I, he's my best friend, not my lover. Never has been."

I breathed deeply. It was a relief to tell him. As much as I tried to busy myself with work, I'd remained anxious all day wanting to talk to him and explain.

"Thank ye for telling me, lass. May I ask ye one more question?"

I nodded, feeling sleepy now that my previous anxiety melted away.

"Then why did ye and Jeffrey almost marry?"

"Oh. Gosh." I rubbed my eyelids with my thumb and middle finger. My almost-marriage to Jeffrey seemed so much like a bad dream that it still didn't seem real to me. "My father had taken a liking to Jeffrey once he saw what a great father he was to Cooper and talked him into going to law school. He even paid for it. Once Jeffrey graduated, he made him a partner at his law firm. And then he decided that just wasn't good enough, so he blackmailed us. He said it wasn't right for a partner at his firm to have a child and not be married. We went along with it, right up until the wedding day. But we couldn't do it. The real kicker is that Jeffrey doesn't even want to be a lawyer. He did that for me, too, because my father expected it of him."

"I doona think I am fond of yer father, lass."

I snorted. "Join the club."

Eoghanan stood, moving toward the door. It wasn't what I expected, for him to hear my explanation and leave so soon, but I was quickly learning that he was anything but predictable. "Can ye stand up for me, lass?"

I did, stepping toward him. "Why?"

"We were interrupted last evening, aye?"

Hesitantly, I moved closer. My chest all fluttery once again. "Yes."

"Do ye think we should be interrupted again?"

I closed my eyes for a long second, allowing the trickle of anticipation to travel along my spine. "No. Cooper's with his dad."

He reached me in one long step and yanked me toward him with his left hand, pressing the front of my body flush against his chest. I moaned as he kissed me, a slow, sensual kiss that washed away every other thought outside of his touch. My body followed him easily, my mouth opening when his tongue sought entry, my back arching as his hand moved to my breast.

We kissed until both of us were weak limbed and needy. Just when we were on the brink of taking it further, he pulled away, moving quickly to open the door.

"I'll leave ye, lass. 'Tis no the time for more."

I nodded, agreeing on an intellectual basis, but my body screaming with unspoken disappointment. "Right. You're right, though I wish that you weren't."

"Ach, I wish the same." He turned away from me and began his trek down the hall. "Sleep well, lass, for I know that I willna do so."

Chapter 16

I don't know if it was relief at having things sorted out with Eoghanan or my subconscious taking advantage of the fact that having Jeffrey here relieved me from having to be on constant Cooper watch, but I slept later than usual and woke feeling utterly relaxed.

After a quick shower and a messy hair job, I walked downstairs to find everyone visiting happily in the living room. This time Cooper had roped Jerry into getting down onto the floor with him. I silently worried about the old man's knees, though he didn't seem the least bit bothered by them as he dramatically role-played with Coop's dinosaurs.

"Mom! I thought you were gonna sleep all day, lazy head." Pausing their game, he ran to greet me. I scooped him up in my arms, kissing him firmly on the top of his head.

"All day? I might have slept a little later. It's only eight in the morning. What time did you get up?"

"Oh, I don't know, the usual time."

"I know." Jeffrey turned to answer me, his eyes still sleepy, rounded out by dark circles. Clearly, Cooper hadn't given his father the same courtesy he usually gave me by occupying himself for a while. "It was four. Four a.m., and he's jacked up like he had six cups of coffee."

I played with Coop's messy curls as I sat him back down on his feet. "Well, if that really is the usual time, I never did set my alarm that early. I truly don't know how you do it, Coop."

He shrugged, looking up at me with a grin. "I don't know, Mom, I really don't. I guess I'm just too excited for all the things I gotta do each day to sleep."

I laughed, it was a beautiful attitude; I hoped he'd keep it always. "I guess so." I turned my attention to everyone else in the room, catching Eoghanan's eye for the first time this morning.

He smiled at me, but not widely enough so as to draw attention from everyone else. His eyes said more, nearly as tired as Jeffrey's but excited and happy. I hadn't felt that way in such a long time—that feeling of being in a room with many people, but being so intensely aware of just one person that it's as if there's a secret between you that no one knows. The promise of another encounter if you can just find the time to sneak away together. I hoped that the opportunity would come for us, very soon.

Eventually, I pulled my eyes away and willed myself to speak, addressing the room as a whole. "What's on everybody's agenda? How about we all drive to McMillan Castle and explore around there for the day?"

"McMillan Castle? Why there, lass?" Eoghanan seemed shocked by my suggestion, though I couldn't imagine why.

"For the article. It looks lovely on the Internet, and I'd like to check it out. Do you know it?"

"Aye." Eoghanan shared a knowing glance with Morna, puzzling me further. "I know it verra well, lass. 'Tis a good way from here."

"Farther than Edinburgh?" I couldn't begin to rationalize his reaction. As much time as he'd spent in the inn, I'd expected him to jump at any excuse to get out for awhile. Instead, he seemed genuinely hesitant. Even more than that really, he seemed afraid to go there.

"No, 'tis closer than Edinburgh."

"Is it haunted or something?" I laughed, but his face showed he didn't think me funny.

"No for ye, though it might be for meself." He said it softly, almost underneath his breath.

I wasn't given the chance to ask him what he meant by that, for as soon as he spoke, Morna leapt up from the couch, interrupting.

"I think it's a lovely idea, Grace. We should leave soon, for it isna a short ride. Cooper," she tapped him gently on the shoulder, "would ye mind helping me make some sandwiches to pack? Jerry, why doona ye and Jeffrey ready the cars? Grace, ye go pack yer camera."

Everyone dispersed quickly, and I was left with little choice but to do the same. I hesitated, lingering in the doorway until it was only Eoghanan and me in the living room. "Are you okay?"

He nodded, standing and moving forward to grab my hand, squeezing it gently. "Aye. McMillan Castle is lovely. 'Tis only..." he hesitated far too long, finally releasing my hand as he turned away, ending the conversation. "Never mind, lass. Go and get yer things. 'Tis nothing to worry yerself over."

Knowing when to leave well enough alone, I stepped away, wondering all the way to my room just what had been said during the other conversation in the living room.

The conversation that had been entirely silent.

* * *

Eoghanan wanted to tell her desperately just why he didn't wish to go to McMillan Castle. That he didn't wish to see his home, the castle he'd grown up in, crawling with visitors, no longer a home or safe haven among the Highlands. All of it a painful reminder that while he knew his family lived in the past, in today's time they'd all been dead for hundreds of years.

A hand gripped his shoulder, pulling him from his thoughts. Morna stood next to him, her knowing eyes telling him she already knew his concerns.

"Ye needn't worry. I too once had trouble visiting me old home. But now, seeing all that it is today gives me comfort that harm dinna befall all those I love over the centuries. McMillan Castle is still in fine condition today; ye will be surprised to find that many things still look much the same. And…" she patted his right hand, where he gripped the spelled rock that had sent him here. "If ye are worried that I'll spell ye back, I have no intention of doing so today. No, when ye are just getting to know the lass. Besides, ye still need to heal, and ye have some time before Mitsy's babe is born."

"Thank ye," Eoghanan turned the rock over in his hand, realizing that perhaps leaving had been his greatest fear. He couldn't go home just yet, not before he'd told Grace the truth.

Smiling, she stepped toward the hallway. "Still, I think it best ye leave the wee rock here. Ye wouldna want someone throwing it into the pond by happenchance."

"No, I wouldna."

Morna turned to leave as he placed the rock down, and he called out to stop her. "Morna, will she believe me?"

"Grace? Ye care verra much about the lass, aye?"

Eoghanan nodded. "Aye, far too much and too soon as well."

"There is no such thing as too soon if 'tis a match that is destined. While Grace doesna know it yet, ye do, I can tell. 'Tis destined, lad, so though she might need some help, when ye decide to tell her, she'll believe ye in time.

* * *

Cooper couldn't see them, but he listened attentively, his back flat against the side of the kitchen wall. *Please don't let Mom catch me. Please don't let Mom catch me.* He repeated the words over and over again in his mind, not wishing to be caught eavesdropping once again.

Waiting until E-o's heavy footsteps walked up the stairs, and Morna's voice hollered after Jerry as she exited the front door, he silently made his way into the living room.

He knew Mom liked E-o. He'd never seen her get dressed up so nice just for dinner. Cooper liked E-o, too. He even thought that maybe Dad liked him all right.

If Mom needed help believing in the magic, then he'd be the perfect helper.

He'd noticed the black, shiny rock E-o had held this morning. Now the rock lay on the small table in the center of the room. Sticking his head out in the hallway and looking both directions for good measure, he scurried quietly over to the table.

Picking up the rock, he slipped it securely away in the pocket of his jeans.

Chapter 17

Eoghanan imagined ghosts felt much the same way when they traveled the halls of their homes, silently watching over loved ones. As he roamed through the empty dining hall now lit with the same electrical hanging lamps that hung from the ceilings of Morna's home, a strange realization hit him— although he couldn't see them, he imagined that his family ate in this very room at much the same time of day—only hundreds of years in the past. They wouldn't know that he stood among them, oblivious of his unseen presence so many years in the future.

Shaking his head to push the nostalgia away, Eoghanan wandered up the stairs to his old bedchamber continuing his search for Cooper as he'd promised the boy he would. Trying to remember what the lad had told him to call in warning, he spoke out to the empty room. "Ready or no, here I come."

The room truly did look much the same, thanks to many rounds of restorations. Red ropes meant to keep visitors away from certain items lined the furnishings, ropes that he and Cooper ignored entirely during their game of hide-and-seek. They were the only visitors at the castle this day, thanks to Morna, so it became their playground.

Eoghanan stepped over the rope to open a chest, not his chest but one much like it, near the end of the bed. Cooper sat crouched down inside.

"Found ye."

"Oh man, I thought this was such a good one. How do you keep finding me?"

Eoghanan looked around to ensure that Grace hadn't

wandered in on them. "Have ye kept our secret, Cooper?"

"About the magic and you being like really, really old and stuff? Yeah, of course I have."

Eoghanan laughed loudly, the sound of it echoing off the walls. "I am no verra old, Cooper. Why do ye think that?"

The young boy held his hands palms up, shrugging a bit as he spoke. "Well, if you can travel in time and you were born close to the dinosaurs, then you're really old."

"No verra close to the dinosaurs, but 'tis no me point. If ye have kept the secret this long, perhaps I can tell ye another, aye?"

"Yeah, I can keep it."

"This castle is where I was born. In me own time, 'tis where I live. This is me own bedchamber."

"Awwwesome. So, when are you gonna tell Mom?"

It was the very question he'd asked himself all day. It seemed the best place, at his home, the place he loved most in the world. "I doona know."

"Don't you like her?"

Eoghanan smiled, taking Cooper by the hand and walking toward the staircase where they sat down next to one another.

"Aye, I like her verra much. 'Tis why I doona know if I should tell her, even though I want to."

Cooper regarded him skeptically. "That doesn't make any sense, E-o."

"Aye, ye may be right. Ye see, we are still verra new to each other, yer mother and I, but I care about her verra much. That doesna mean that she feels the same way. If I did tell her about the magic, 'twould be so that she might consider returning home with me—along with ye and yer father, if ye wish it. She's only known me a week."

"A week is a real long time."

Cooper sat with his elbows on his knees, his palms cupping his small face. He was an intelligent child; fun, curious, kind, and in that moment, Eoghanan knew that he loved him. The boy's presence awakened a desire within him to be a father; a desire he'd not known he'd ever had. If he could love the boy so quickly, after only a week, why couldn't he love the boy's mother as well?

"Do ye really think a week is a long time?"

Eoghanan waited patiently, appreciating how Cooper always took time before answering a question. He thought about things deeply. At such a young age, the boy had already mastered a talent far too few people possessed.

Finally, he spoke. "Well, are we talkin' about love here?"

Eoghanan smiled, nodding silently.

"Then yeah, a week is *real* long. Let me think…when Bebop tells me something I don't understand, he tells me a story to help me get it. You wanna hear a story, E-o?"

"Aye, tell me yer story."

"I don't know if you know this, but next to Mom, Dad, and Bebop, I love dinosaurs more than anything else in the world. I mean," he spread his arms wide. "I love them soooo much, and it didn't take me a week to figure that out. I knew the first time I saw a dinosaur, in a book my Bebop got for me, that I loved them. Not everybody loves dinosaurs. Grandfather doesn't, but that's okay. 'Cause I was *meant* to love dinosaurs. What I mean is, if you are meant to love each other, you and my Mom, then a week is a long time."

Eoghanan shook his head in disbelief. "How old are ye again, Cooper?"

Cooper tapped the side of his head. "I know, I'm kinda weird. I think my brain is older than my body."

He laughed. "I doona doubt it. Ye are verra special lad. I have never met a child like ye before."

"Does that mean you're gonna tell her?"

Eoghanan stood, jerking his head toward the castle's main entrance. "Aye, I think that I shall. Let's go and join the others. Do ye mind staying with yer father a while, so that I may talk to yer mother alone?"

"Yeah, sure. Maybe Dad will play hide-and-seek."

"Aye, perhaps he will. I think it may take some time to explain the magic to her. Even then, I doona know if she will believe me."

Cooper took off down the stairs, hollering at him over his shoulder. "Don't worry about that E-o. I'll help you with that part. If she doesn't believe you, I think I know something that will work."

Eoghanan couldn't explain it, but as Cooper ran out the front door of the castle, a sense of unease settled over him.

Chapter 18

Much to all of our delight, we arrived at McMillan Castle near noon without a tourist to be found. It was literally as if it had been vacated just for us. The only person on the property, as far as I could tell, was a lackadaisical ticket operator who seemed much too interested in her magazine to worry about what areas we did and did not enter. We had free run of the place.

It made for excellent picture taking. While Jerry, Morna, and Jeffrey visited by the pond out front, Eoghanan occupied Coop with a castle-sized game of hide and seek. It was a magnificent edifice, and I was glad to get some work done, but I was even more pleased when Cooper came running out headed straight toward his dad.

Eoghanan made his way out more slowly, lingering near the entryway of the castle. Something within my gut started to hum each time I saw him. I barely knew him, but I kept trying to think of reasons to call Mr. Perdie to ask if I could extend my trip by a week or two. I still had a week left here, but I was beginning to believe that no amount of time would ever feel like enough. It was completely irrational thinking; I didn't know his last name, about his family, what he did for a living, but I knew that after knowing him, even if I left, I would think about him every day for the rest of my life.

Still, that wasn't enough. There was a mystery about him that I couldn't figure out and, until I did, I wouldn't allow myself to trust my feelings for him. I knew myself well enough to know, despite my lack of experience in recent years, that I had a tendency to fall for bad guys—the kind of guys who purposely leave important details about themselves out of the conversation; the kind of guys who are attractive more for their mystery than their substance.

I could tell by Eoghanan's eyes—Cooper and Bebop were right about people's eyes—that he couldn't be lumped into the same "bad guy" group as so many others. Regardless, he still remained more of a mystery than I was comfortable with.

His injury, although partially explained, still made very little sense. Who in the heck got into sword fights nowadays? And what could he possibly have done to provoke it? Not to mention his odd speech and his obvious fascination with the car.

And although I'd put off his reaction to Jeffrey's arrival as being more out of surprise at the situation than true anger, it seemed weird to me that he would assume that just because Jeffrey was Cooper's father that he and I were married. With divorce being so common, it surprised me that it wasn't his first conclusion rather than me being a cheating spouse.

Lastly, Cooper's small mention of a secret between him and Eoghanan nagged at the back of my mind relentlessly. I knew it had to be innocent enough, but I couldn't help but wonder if it was somehow related to Cooper's belief that Eoghanan was the man he'd thought he'd seen at the park and airport. I knew my son, and he was not one to let things go. If he believed something, he wouldn't allow it to be dismissed without proper explanation, and he'd dropped the issue suddenly—right after his fishing trip with Jerry and Eoghanan.

I liked Eoghanan…a lot. I loved talking to him, I loved how much Cooper adored him, and despite how it made me feel like a sex-crazed teenager, I couldn't be near him without daydreaming about him slamming me up against whatever wall, car, or now castle that we stood next to. Still, I needed to know a lot more, and very soon, or I would have no reason to stay past the end of the week—even if he wanted me to, which as of yet, he'd said nothing of the sort.

I smiled as I approached him, hoping he couldn't see all the thoughts running wild behind my eyes. "Hey, you. Everything alright?"

His face was serious and a bit apprehensive as he took my hand and began to pull me away from the others, toward the side of the castle. "Aye, come with me."

Allowing myself one quick glance backward to make sure Cooper was being supervised, I turned back to him, allowing him to lead the way. It struck me as odd that he moved with such direction. Without a doubt, he'd been here before. "Where are we going?"

"There is a tree near the back with a large branch that nearly touches the ground. I go there often to think."

"Often?" How could that be? He'd told me more than once that he lived quite far from Morna and Jerry's. While it was a several hour drive, he'd spoken about his home as if it were much further away. Had he lied and that was why he'd been so hesitant to come here? "Are you from near here?"

He turned suddenly toward me, blocking the path. "Aye, in a way I am from both verra near here and verra far away. Do ye believe in magic, lass?"

What a weird question. I stuttered a little, unsure of what he meant by 'magic.' "Do you mean like a higher power or something? If so, yes, I do. If you mean like hocus pocus stuff, I've not ever seen it, so I would say I don't know. I do think things happen all the time that have no logical explanation, and perhaps those things are the result of a kind of magic. Why?"

Perhaps the magic he spoke of lay within him, for I couldn't help but feel as if he'd read my mind. While the direction of the conversation made me uneasy, I had a feeling I would finally be granted some answers.

He said nothing until we reached the tree. After he sat down, he pulled me in next to him. "I'd like to tell ye something...me surname is McMillan."

"Oh." It seemed an odd build up for such a small piece of information; then I remembered where we were. "Oh. Ooohhh..." each time I said the word a little louder, as if some sort of grand realization came over me...it didn't. "So, you didn't grow up quite as far from the inn as I thought, although I guess that all depends on your perspective. Does your family own this? Your ancestors were what? Scottish lairds or something?"

"Aye, they were, but no only me ancestors. Me brother is Laird of this castle now."

"Your brother." It wasn't so much a question, as a statement while I thought about what he could mean. It was the first I'd heard of a brother. While I supposed there could still be a laird by title if his family did still own the castle, I didn't think it would be anything more than just that…a title. "Okay, so does your family live near here? Sort of oversee things?"

Eoghanan began to cross his arms, but stopped as his shoulder pulled. "We doona live near it. We live in it, lass."

I quickly grew frustrated. I'd taken the same self-guided tour of the place as he had, and it was obvious that no one actually still lived in the castle. Furthermore, if they had, why hadn't he said anything while we were walking through it? Told us stories, or talked about the castle's history, his ancestors, anything?

"Eoghanan, I walked through that castle just a few hours ago, and there's no one living there now."

Eoghanan stood and started pacing back and forth in front of me. He looked as frustrated as I felt. "Do ye remember what Cooper said about me when ye first arrived here?"

I pulled my jacket around me more snugly. There was little wind, but my body temperature seemed to drop suddenly. "Which part? When he mistook you for someone else? He thought he saw you at the airport, but obviously that wasn't you."

"Aye, lass. It was."

* * *

Cooper ran up to his dad, who stood by the pond, waving at Morna and Jerry as they pulled away from the castle.

101

"Where are they going?"

"They're just heading back a little early so that Morna can get started on some dinner. We'll ride back with Eoghanan and your Mom whenever they get back over here."

Cooper reached down into his pocket, turning the stone over and over, thinking about the magic. It was taking Mom and E-o too long. E-o had been right; his Mom was too much of a grown-up to believe. He would have to help her.

He pulled out the stone, trying to remember what he'd heard Morna say. He couldn't remember exactly, but it was something about the rock touching water. If the rock was magical, his Mom would be angry with him for sure, but it was the only way to show her. Besides, it might not do anything— just like the colored dinosaur eggs his Dad had gotten him once. They were supposed to hatch if placed in water, but they never did.

If only grown-ups were easier to teach things to, he wouldn't have had to take the rock in the first place. Rearing back, he let the rock fly; everything went black the moment it hit the water.

Chapter 19

"Uh, I'm sorry, can you say that again?" Obviously, he'd misspoken. There was absolutely no way he'd been in the airport. Jerry and Morna had both said Eoghanan had been at their inn for several months. He didn't strike me as the type of man who would take off for a quick little "vaca" to New York.

"Grace, I know that ye willna believe me. No until ye witness it for yerself. 'Tis my hope that ye will allow me to tell ye all that I know and then consider allowing me to prove it to ye."

"Witness what? Eoghanan, you're freaking me out. Just say whatever it is you're trying to say, plainly. Get on with it."

"I was injured by a sword, just as I told ye, but 'twas no in this time. This wound," he paused to point at the scar that started on the side of his temple. "was given to me in the year sixteen hundred and forty-seven, in the verra castle behind ye. I am only in this time now, so that I can heal with the help of Morna's magic."

"Alright." I stood, tossing a hand in dismissal toward him as I took off back toward the pond. "I've had enough. You're cra…"

The word hung unfinished, my feet taking off the moment I saw Jeffrey running toward us, dripping wet, breathless and screaming for me to follow him. He turned back toward the direction he'd come as soon as he saw me running, screaming at me from over his shoulder.

"Grace, I…Cooper's gone."

"What do you mean, he's gone?" My stomach churned, vomit threatening to come up at the panic that built within me.

"I don't know, Grace. He was standing right there. Right there, Grace." He pointed at the grass next to me. He was crying now, tears flowing freely, his voice a panicked rasp. "I was right next to him. He just threw a rock. I swear. I didn't turn away from him for a second. He just threw a rock and…" he shook his head as if he didn't believe his own words, "he just vanished."

"Jeffrey, if Cooper put you up to this and you were stupid enough to go along with it, I swear to you, I will murder you."

"Grace!" He grabbed me roughly, shaking me so hard my teeth rattled. "Do I look like I'm joking?"

He didn't, not at all, and my brain simply couldn't process the horror of what he said. "He's gone."

"No. No, no, no, no, no, no, no." I could say nothing else as I collapsed against him.

"Hush, lass." Eoghanan stood behind me, pulling me off of Jeffrey. He gripped my shoulders too tightly, but it was enough to make me do as he said. "Jeffrey, show me what the lad did."

He was so calm I wanted to slap him. I twisted away from his grip, whirling on him, my voice barely forming words— like in a dream where you want to scream, you need to scream, but it just won't come.

"What's…what's the matter with you? We don't have time. We have to find him."

I jumped toward the water to search for him, but Eoghanan reached out, jerking me back against him with his left hand, wrapping it around my waist so that I couldn't move.

"Jeffrey, pick up a damn rock and show me what the lad did."

Eoghanan's tone was deeper than I'd ever heard it. It was a direct order.

I struggled against him, but he held me still as Jeffrey looked at him, confusion and shock muddling his normally flawless face. Slowly, he bent to pick up a rock. Shaking his head, he held his hand back, "He just…all he did was throw it."

Jeffrey's rock went sailing toward the water. When it hit

the surface and disappeared below the water, so did Jeffrey.

I screamed. Something hard hit me on the top of the head causing my vision to blur. The last thing I saw before I lost consciousness was the sight of headlights barreling toward us.

Chapter 20

"What in the blethering hell did ye do to her, Morna?"

My eyes remained closed, and though I tried to open them, they wouldn't budge. The same could be said for every other part of my body. Someone must have sedated me for I couldn't lift my arms or legs, open my eyes, speak. I could do nothing but listen to all that they said.

"Calm down, Eoghanan, I just put her to sleep for a while. We wouldna have been able to get her in the car, otherwise."

"Ye needed to explain to her what happened, no kidnap the lass."

I could feel Eoghanan running his hand through my hair, and I knew that I lay slumped against him.

"Kidnap her?" Morna's voice sounded appalled at the suggestion. "Doona ye blame me for this mess. I told ye no to bring the rock, dinna I?"

"Aye, and I did leave it. Cooper must have picked it up behind me. I thought that ye had to skip the rock for it take ye back. Surely the lad couldna do that."

Cooper. His name jolted my memory of all that had happened, and I knew I was more than just physically sedated. I knew my son was gone. I'd seen Jeffrey vanish before me, yet the panic I knew I should be feeling wouldn't come. I felt eerily at peace, unworried, sleepy. I fought the urge to sleep, listening intently to try and understand.

"Aye, 'tis usually true, but I made the stone to allow those that needed to travel the ability to do so. Cooper must be meant to travel back if it allowed him to simply throw it and no skip it, nor float it like ye did."

"What about Jeffrey?" It was Jerry's voice, speaking up for the first time.

"Ach, ye saw how quickly I turned the car around. I felt it the moment Cooper traveled back and immediately spelled the other rocks so that someone could follow him."

"How did ye know one of us would throw it?" Eoghanan's voice again.

"I dinna know, 'twas all I could think to do until we got to ye."

"Aye, fine. When ye reached us, why dinna ye send Grace and me back right away?"

All of this talk of 'back' made little sense, but I was unable to ask questions.

"Eoghanan, ye know that ye are in no shape to travel so far back yet. Grace's arrival has delayed yer progress. We have no been working at it consistently."

"It no longer matters if I am ready or no. Grace willna wait for me to heal to get to her son, and I willna let her go back without me."

"Aye, I know. 'Tis why I dinna send ye back there. If ye must go, which aye, I know that ye must, I will at least make sure that ye are as tended to as best ye can be before making the journey. Now, rest yer eyes a while, lad, we've much to do when we get back to me home."

As their voices quieted, so did my strength to stay awake. I allowed sleep to take me, hoping as I drifted that when next I woke I would be able to feel something other than the unsettling calm.

* * *

"Alright, lass, time for ye to wake up now."

Morna's voice called to me from beside my bed. Slowly my eyelids flickered open.

I lay in my bed at the inn with Jerry sitting at its end, Eoghanan on my right side rubbing my hand gently, and

Morna on my left side regarding me closely.

I concentrated on trying to open my mouth, pleased to find that motion had returned to it. After stretching my jaw a moment, I spoke. "You all need to tell me exactly what is going on. Where is my son?" While I could move my body, I still felt just as calm as before, and I hated it. Intellectually knowing that something was very wrong, but not being able to feel that emotion disturbed me greatly.

"Aye, 'tis exactly what we intend to do. Ye may notice that ye feel a bit calm, 'tis only something that I've done so ye will sit still long enough to hear everything. It will recede slowly, but if ye lose yer cool, Grace, I'll spell ye again."

"Spell me?" My tone came off as sarcastic, though after everything, I wasn't all that inclined to disbelieve her.

"Aye, lass. Spell ye. I'm a witch and quite a powerful one." Morna extended a glass of water in my direction, and I took it, sitting up in the bed.

"'Tis what I meant to tell ye, when..." Eoghanan trailed off.

My thoughts went right back to Cooper and Jeffrey. "Where are they?"

Eoghanan was nervous. I could tell by the way he kept fumbling with my fingers, though I didn't understand why since, for the time being, I wouldn't get upset no matter what he said. I was entirely incapable of it. As soon as I could feel again, I knew I would be spitfire angry at being repressed in such a manner.

"They're still at McMillan Castle with me family, in the seventeenth century."

I nodded skeptically. "Of course they are. So Morna is a witch, you're a time traveler," I turned my eyes on Jerry. "What are you? A goblin?"

The old man frowned at me, "I take offense to that, lass. Do I look like a goblin?"

I didn't answer him, instead looking at Eoghanan for

further explanation.

"'Tis like I told ye, Grace. I was only sent here after I almost died. Me brother is married to a lass from this time; her name is Mitsy. Morna sent her back as well. When I was injured, she knew that Morna could save me and sent me forward to her."

"Okay," I couldn't argue with him. No matter how ridiculous it sounded, no matter how unbelievable, I had seen Jeffrey vanish. There was no doubt in my mind about that. "So why were you in the airport? And the park? Before Jeffrey...you said that Cooper was right about seeing you. Have you been stalking us?"

"No." It was Morna who answered, rising quickly to Eoghanan's defense. "Of course he has no been stalking ye. 'Twas me that sent him to ye."

She glanced over at Eoghanan, speaking to him for a moment. "Aye, ye heard me. I lied to ye. I do control where ye go on yer travels."

Returning her attention to me, she continued. "The span of time between now and his home was too great with his wound. The spell rips ye apart a bit,"

I swallowed, thinking of Cooper, grateful for the first time that I couldn't feel anything.

Eoghanan must have been able to follow my train of thought, for he interrupted Morna thumbing my hand comfortingly. "Do ye really think that is what ye needed to tell her just now? With her worried about wee Cooper?"

Morna nodded, dismissing him. "Aye, she needed to know so I could explain why ye dinna go straight home. Besides, she is no worried about anything at the moment." I hated that she was right. "Back to what I was saying to ye, lass. I have been slowly building his strength in the travel, though it seems there is no more time for that. I know that ye are ready to see that yer boy is well. In just a moment, I will remove the spell from ye, and we will prepare Eoghanan right away."

"Prepare him?" After Morna's description, I could just imagine Eoghanan being ripped apart, only to have his fragile skin not come back together properly. "If he's not ready, I can go by myself. I just want to make sure Cooper is okay. I don't want," I looked at Eoghanan. "I don't want you getting hurt. I can go alone."

He kissed my hand gently and reached up to brush a lock of hair out of my eyes. "Ye are mad if ye think I would let ye do that, lass. I'm going."

Morna stood abruptly, nodding as she waved to Jerry so that he'd follow her out the door. "As I thought. Eoghanan, stay with the lass and help her once I lift the spell. When she's composed herself, both of ye come and find me. We will do the spell tonight."

I had one brief moment of confusion where I wondered why I would need help, then the spell lifted. Everything—my panic over my son being gone, my shock at watching Jeffrey disappear, my disbelief that apparently magic existed in the world, my worry over Eoghanan—it all hit me at once.

As Morna and Jerry left us, closing the door behind them, I collapsed into a fit of sobs.

Chapter 21

I didn't cry long. I couldn't allow myself to waste time that way when all I wanted to do was use Morna's hocus pocus to get my son back. I didn't want to cry at all, but as soon as she lifted the spell, I couldn't help it; the sudden rush of so many emotions sent me into a sort of mini-hysteria, and I gasped and cried and screamed in quick succession.

I allowed myself five minutes of good, uncontrollable panic. Then I stood from the bed, swallowing all of it.

"Ok, I'm ready."

"Grace," Eoghanan twisted me so that I faced him. "I promise ye that he's safe."

"Don't." I wrenched from his grasp, knowing that if he tried to comfort me, I'd start crying again. He looked as if I'd slapped him. I made haste to apologize, walking toward him and standing up on the tip of my toes, kissing him gently.

It was the only intimate act between us since our first kiss and rather than the raw heat that had flooded my body last time, the touch of his kiss calmed me, comforted me in a way I'd never experienced before. I realized in that instant that it didn't matter how little I knew about him, how short the time that we'd known one another—whatever this was between us—it was right.

"I'm sorry," I said, wrapping my arms around him, allowing my head to lean against his chest. "It's just, I'll lose it again if we talk about it. I don't understand any of this and it…it scares me." I let go and took half a step away from him. "Everything scares me right now. Cooper. Jeffrey. Morna. This…" I touched my chest and then his and he grasped my hand, holding it in place against his chest.

"Ach lass, I have never been so frightened in me life. I know that ye canna understand all of this, no yet, but ye will when ye see it. I know that ye canna help but worry about Cooper, but Morna wouldna let harm come to him and neither would me family. He and Jeffrey are both safe, I'd stake me life on it."

I nodded, sniffling as I tried to keep from crying again. "I just need him back."

"I know. Let's go to him, aye?"

I wanted to leave immediately, to let Morna spell me and send me hurtling back through time toward my son, but I couldn't get Eoghanan's wound out of my mind.

"Eoghanan, Morna said that she'd slowly been building your strength to travel back, that the time between now and your home was too far for you yet. What does that mean? It's your skin, isn't it? It's still not healed well enough."

"Aye, but I'll do me best to survive it. The first time Morna sent me back, she sent me to the park where I saw ye and Cooper. When she pulled me back here, me wound split open and bled verra badly."

"Yeah, I figured it was something like that. Nope. Sorry." I pulled away, opening the door and leaving to search for Morna. I spoke as he followed me. "There is no way in hell that I am letting you go back with me. The park wasn't that long ago. What do you think will happen to you if you're sent back multiple centuries?"

"I doona care. I willna allow ye to go without me." He grabbed my arm and spun me toward him, gripping me tightly.

"You won't allow me?"

"No, and Morna willna allow it either."

Jerking away from him, I called for her. "Morna, I'm ready to go. Eoghanan is staying here."

"No. I willna do it, lass." He wasn't screaming like I was; he said it quietly, calmly, completely unflustered by the possibility of his imminent death.

"He's right. I willna spell ye back unless he goes with ye." Morna appeared suddenly in the hallway, spools of medicinal cloth in her arms.

"What if it kills him? What is all that for?"
Morna shook her head, clearly annoyed, and held them up in Eoghanan's direction.

"Ye must think that I am no a verra good witch. I willna let the lad die. Now. Come with me."

"How would I know what kind of witch you are? I didn't even know witches actually existed until today."

She ignored me, instead leading us into Eoghanan's room where she'd stripped the bed of its blankets, leaving only a sheet. "Eoghanan, strip yer clothes. I will bind ye up so that when the scar rips open, at least it will be held in place when ye come back together." She glanced over at me briefly. "Give him some privacy, unless ye wish to see every inch of him."

Eoghanan laughed, "She's already seen me. Still," he winked at me, "perhaps ye might want to step out just a moment."

* * *

Morna called me back inside nearly thirty minutes later. No matter how un-funny the situation, the sight of Eoghanan wrapped up like a mummy had Morna smiling with unexpressed laughter.

"What's the matter with the both of you? You don't even know if this is going to work."

"Doona worry, it will work. I've made a special salve to place upon it. As long as the bandages are no removed for a few days, it should do the trick. 'Tis something I could have done to him much earlier, but he needed to remain here a while longer, even if he dinna know it at the time."

"Why's that?" Everyone—Eoghanan, Cooper, Jeffrey— they all seemed to adore Morna. I wasn't quite there yet. She was too cryptic and had a penchant for meddling that had turned everything I thought I knew about the world, and my own life, upside down.

"If he'd left when he could've, he wouldna have met ye, lass. At least thank me for that, for whether ye are ready to say it yet or no, ye know well enough that the two of ye are a fine match."

I couldn't very well argue with that. She was right, but it still left me feeling awkward and shy. I fumbled for something else to say. "Why didn't you just stitch him?"

"I am a witch, no a seamstress. I'm too squeamish to go about sewing him up from head to toe. Are ye ready?"

She didn't wait for me to answer, moving quickly on from the end of her question to muttering words I couldn't understand.

Eoghanan reached for my hand. I took it gladly as pain started to radiate through my body.

"Doona let go, lass. 'Twill all be over soon."

Chapter 22

"Mooommmm….Moooommmm…"

Some part of my brain registered the word, drawn out as if it were in a song each time. My head ached something dreadful, and I couldn't remember what I'd been doing an hour ago or where I was now.

I racked my brain for the answer. When it came to me I threw myself forward, opening my eyes as he pounced on me, throwing his little arms around my neck. "Cooper!" The movement jarred my head. With my arms still wrapped around him, I grabbed my forehead, willing the throbbing to stop.

"Aye, I havena experienced it meself, but me wife says the ache in yer head is the worst part. At least ye dinna land in the pond." I opened my eyes to see a man slightly taller than Eoghanan, clad in a kilt, with dark hair and brooding eyes in front of me.

Eoghanan sat up next to me. Blood seeped through the cloth wound around him. "I doona wish to argue with ye, but 'tis no me head that hurts."

I shifted, swinging Cooper's weight onto my side so that I could lean over and check on him. "You are a stupid, stupid man. You should not have come."

"'Tis no nearly as bad as I expected, lass. Morna said it might bleed a little."

He struggled to stand, and the tall man reached out a hand to assist him. Once he was standing, I could see that he was right. He only bled a little.

My nerves relaxed and I stood up, Cooper still clinging to my hip.

"Are you okay?" I reached up and brushed his hair back, examining his head for apparent injury, just like every mom in every TV movie did when she found her missing child. I realized that it was a pointless gesture and stopped, settling instead for planting a big kiss on the top of his head.

"Yeah, Mom, I'm awesome! Everything is lit by candles, and I got to pee in a bucket! Even the bathtub is just a big old bucket that they carry into your room. I only wish that they had dragons. I really thought there would be some here." His voice drifted a little as he reflected on his disappointment.

I heard footsteps approaching and another voice joined the conversation. I turned to see Jeffrey walking along with a stunning red head, her belly swollen with the later months of pregnancy. I moved to hug Jeffrey as she spoke to me.

"You must be Grace. I'm Mitsy." She extended a hand, which I took, and she continued. "I have some ibuprofen for your head that should help. I know it's got to be hurting you. The time travel thing is a bitch." She quickly glanced down at Cooper who snorted slightly at the word. She began apologizing profusely. "Gosh, I'm sorry. I have a tendency to speak without thinking." She patted her stomach. "Poor kid. I am so not ready for this."

The man who stood next to Eoghanan, the man whose name I still didn't know, reached over to grab the woman's hand, pulling her into him. "No one is ever ready, but ye will be a wonderful mother."

"He's very right. You can't be ready, not really, until the baby is here. Even then, you're just learning as you go. Um...you have ibruprofen?"

Mitsy laughed, nodding excitedly. "Yes, Morna often sends modern-ish things to Conall Castle for Bri, and I grabbed some the last time I was there."

"Oh." I didn't know who Bri was, but I didn't ask.

"Grace." Eoghanan stepped closer to me, placing a hand on the small of my back. "This is me brother, Baodan. He is

Laird here at McMillan Castle, and ye have already met Mitsy, for she has better manners and has already introduced herself."

Mitsy laughed and threw her arms around Eoghanan. She clung to him despite his bandages, and he gladly embraced her. I could sense the strong friendship between them. I expected that their relationship was part of the reason he'd not questioned my relationship with Jeffrey once he'd calmed down and allowed me to explain it to him.

"I'm so glad you're back, E-o." Her voice was soft and near cracking, but she held back her tears.

She'd called him E-o, just like Cooper, and I realized that Mitsy was the beloved 'girlfriend' he'd mentioned. I really needed to teach him the definition of that word.

"I've been so worried about you. I mean, I trusted Morna to take care of you, but…I still can't believe you did that. You're a stupid, stupid man."

Eoghanan laughed loudly, prying Mitsy off of him. "I doona think I like that word. I've been called it too many times today."

"What did he do?" My question seemed to interrupt their moment a little, but I wanted to know. In this time, a sword injury made much more sense, but Eoghanan's previous description of the event had been much too vague.

"Oh," Mitsy gave Eoghanan a look that said she was surprised I didn't already know. "Their brother was a crazy sociopath who murdered anyone who inconvenienced him. He tried to do the same to me, but Eoghanan jumped in the way of the sword. Then I killed the bastard." She looked at Cooper apologetically once again. "Sorry."

Cooper waved a hand dismissively. He'd heard his Grandfather curse plenty.

"Oh." I was saying that word a lot lately. She'd explained it only a fraction better than Eoghanan, and it did nothing to satisfy my curiosity. I looked over in Eoghanan's direction and decided further probing could wait. He'd wilted a bit and now

117

stood leaning harshly onto his left foot. He looked like he might fall over at any moment.

Cooper must have noticed the same thing, and he squirmed in my arms so that I would set him down. He ran over to Eoghanan's side, leaning against his left leg as if trying to prop him up. "Hey, you don't look so good, E-o. You alright?"

Eoghanan placed a hand on the top of Cooper's head. He tried to smile at him, but it didn't reach his eyes. He started to grow paler with each passing second.

"I'm verra tired. I think we should go inside. Baodan, would ye help me to me chambers?"

Baodan was at his side in an instant, propping him up against his shoulder. Baodan smiled back at his wife—a silent conversation where I was sure he'd asked her to see to the rest of us. Once Baodan and Eoghanan were inside the castle, Mitsy spoke.

"You're lucky you got an explanation before you showed up here. Jeffrey had a bit of a meltdown."

"I did not." He attempted to argue, but his eyes were still glazed over with lingering shock.

Mitsy nodded. *"Definite meltdown,"* she mouthed the words silently to me, smiling before speaking aloud once again. "Anyway, once we got him settled down, he and Cooper spent most of the night exploring the place. I think they'll be fine if we leave them on their own. I'm in desperate need of some modern-day girl talk."

Chapter 23

"Hey, stranger." I stepped inside Eoghanan's chamber for the first time, three days after we'd arrived. I'd kept my distance hoping that without a distraction, he'd be more apt to stay in bed and rest.

At least, this is the reason I told myself so I wouldn't feel guilty. Truthfully, I'd taken advantage of his need to rest by giving myself time to think.

All of it was true—the fact that Morna was a witch, her ability to send those she wished hurtling through time—I could no longer deny any of it. And now, I had to accept what that meant.

Nothing more could ever happen between Eoghanan and me.

I'd hoped that a few days away from him would allow me to gain some perspective. That after wandering around the castle and observing all of the strange differences between this time and my own that I would feel out of place, ready to return home.

I didn't feel that way at all.

I loved it here—the simplicity, the inaccessibility of it. I knew if it was only myself I could stay here forever. All of the castle, as well as Eoghanan's family, could not be more warm and kind. Accustomed to strange, time-traveling Americans, due to Mitsy and Bri who I'd yet to meet, we'd settled in quite nicely among them.

Cooper seemed to love it as well. He used the castle as a sort of massive playground, determined to discover every secret nook and passageway. Jeffrey, I thought, looked at it as a vacation. After years of working the grind of a law firm, he reveled in being able to do what he considered "manly" tasks like horseback riding and learning how to shoot an arrow.

Still, it was easy for them to enjoy the changes for a short amount of time, an impossibility to ask them to do it forever.

I'd set my mind to speaking to Eoghanan about this, to explaining to him that the three of us would need to return home soon. I walked into his room and, after greeting him, took in the droopy, glazed, plastered look on his face.

"Grace, lass." He said my name slowly. He was drunk, I could tell by his droopy eyes, but he wasn't so drunk yet that he'd lost his concern for his own behavior. He didn't want me to know that he was drunk.

"I apologize for this, lass. 'Tis me own doing, not his."

It was Baodan's voice, and I turned toward it. "Why?"

"'Tis time to remove his bandages, but the blood has dried the cloth to him. When I went to remove the bandages from the side of his face…" he paused, "I doona think he screamed like that when the blade tore through him. I thought it best to give him something to dull the pain so that the rest of the removal may not be so painful."

"Ah, good idea. Do you need me to leave? I can come back later."

"No, doona leave, Grace." Eoghanan called to me, swinging his feet over the side of the bed to try and stand. "I'd like for ye to remove them from me."

Baodan gave me no chance to answer him, moving across the room to push his brother back down on the bed. "Ye doona truly wish that lad. When ye are sober, ye will regret asking it of her."

Eoghanan persisted. "Aye, I do wish it. I am no all that drunk, Baodan. Now, leave us be."

Baodan retreated from Eoghanan's side, but lingered in front of me a moment, a question in his eyes.

"I don't mind. Really, we'll be fine."

Nodding once, Baodan left, closing the door behind him. As I walked toward Eoghanan, he smiled a lazy smile that made my insides flutter. I'd yet to see such an unrestrained grin from him. He usually thought too much to appear this relaxed. It was an incredibly endearing look.

I had a sneaking suspicion the conversation I needed to have with him wouldn't happen today.

"Are you sure you want me to do this? I'm not really qualified. I'm not a witch or a nurse, so…"

I now stood right next to his bed, and he reached up and pulled me down so that I sat on its edge. "Aye, lass. Yer hands will be far more gentle than me brother's."

"Okay," I ran my fingertips over the exposed scar that ran down the side of his face. Whatever Morna had placed upon it had altered the skin completely. Only days before the line had been red, angry, relatively new. Now its shade was a close match to the rest of his skin and had the look of a much older scar. It had healed as much as it ever would. "It looks so much better, Eoghanan."

"Aye?"

I couldn't tell if he'd heard a word I said. His eyes were closed, and he was enjoying the feel of my fingertips as they trailed his face. When they reached the base of his neck where the remaining wrap started, he grabbed my hand, bringing it up to his lips and kissed my palm.

"I love yer hands, lass, and the way ye make me feel when ye touch me. Do ye remember when ye cut me hair?" His words were slow, slightly slurred, and incredibly sexy.

"Yes, I do. What about it?"

He still gripped my hand, trailing slow kisses up my arm as he spoke. "All I could think of was what these hands of yers would feel like digging into me shoulders as I claimed ye, pushing meself deeper and deeper inside ye. How ye would shudder beneath me…"

"Okay…" I jerked away, standing up as fast as I could, doing a strange little dance where I shook out my hands and hopped from foot to foot to clear my head and the disastrous thoughts that were flooding it as he spoke. "I think you are further into the bottle than you think, mister. Whether you thought it or not, you would never say that out loud to me sober."

He smiled, getting up from the bed so that he stood in front of me, smiling that same lazy grin. "Aye, mayhap so, Grace, though every word is the truth."

For the moment I was glad that the majority of his body was still wrapped up tightly, but I was about to have to unwrap him like some sort of man candy present, and if he didn't stop talking, I worried I might jump him and beg him to do to me just exactly what he'd imagined.

"Are you ready to get started?" I didn't allow him the chance to answer, gripping the top of the fabric near his neck, tugging to test out just how tightly it was bound. "Does that hurt?"

"No, no in the way that me face did."

I nodded, continuing to pull at the bandage, "Good. I'm going to keep going then."

He said nothing. For the following minutes I worked quietly, pulling and then reaching around him to gather the fabric, repeating the motion over and over. He didn't scream, didn't wince, he simply watched me so intently that tension began to build quite evidently in the room. Each time I leaned forward to wind the cloth around his back, I was tempted to linger.

I wanted nothing more than for him to grab me, kiss me, and take me to his bed, but my rational mind told me to keep to my work. No matter how much I wanted to tell that rational voice in my head to go hang, I inevitably had to leave here; it would be foolish to complicate things further.

"Where have ye been, Grace?"

The question caught me off guard. Despite the fact that I feigned ignorance, I knew exactly what he meant. "What do you mean? I've been right here."

"No, ye have been anywhere but right here, lass. Ye have

plans to leave."

He didn't ask it as a question, and his keen observation caused my hand to still for a brief moment. I'd unwound him to the bottom of his waist. All that was left was his right leg, but I hesitated to go further. I didn't imagine he had on boxer briefs beneath the wrapping.

"I…" I couldn't very well lie to him. Of course I had plans to leave. "I don't really have a choice. There's only a few more days before I'm due back in New York."

"New York. Do ye mean for yer article?" He reached behind himself to grab the roll of bandages I held. "Put them down, lass. Stand up and look at me." After pulling me to my feet, he continued, "Yer magazine will receive the money promised to them with or without yer article. The mysterious benefactor…I believe 'twas Jerry."

Of course it was. "How do you know about that?"

"The telephone 'twas right outside me bedchamber. I heard him speaking to yer boss, though I dinna understand it until the evening when ye told me about yer job."

The telephone. I had a sudden flashback to my phone conversation with my sister and the noise I thought I'd heard behind his door. "The telephone…you heard me, huh?"

He smiled, reaching up with his right hand to tuck some hair behind my ear. The movement in his shoulder was much improved. "Aye, though I could only hear ye, no whoever ye spoke with."

"My sister."

He nodded, "I thought as much." Smiling with one half of his mouth, he released my arms and leaned down to unwrap his lower waist and leg.

I could see the cloth dropping from my peripherals, but I kept my eyes upward, determined not to look at him. It would be my undoing.

In a matter of moments he was naked, but much to my gratitude, he wrapped a blanket around his waist, sitting back

123

down on the bed. He reached for my hand and I joined him, looking at him with sympathy. He held his liquor relatively well, but he'd not feel good tomorrow.

"How does it feel? The scar?"

"I feel like meself for the first time since it happened. I canna believe Morna allowed me to lay there for so long when she could have healed it in a couple of days; though I know now why she did."

That look in his eyes was back; the same look that would never show itself so boldly had he been sober.

"Why's that?"

"Why do ye think, lass?" He kissed me, a hard, rough, consuming kiss so different from what I'd expect from him.

Whether it was the new freedom of movement he had or the loosening of his inhibitions from the alcohol, I didn't know, but he quickly pushed me backward onto the bed, trailing kisses down my neck, dipping his tongue into the crevice between my breasts.

"Eoghanan." His name came breathless on my lips. My breasts were rising and falling at a rapid rate, reaching up to meet his kisses, to accept his tongue.

"Hush, Grace."

He slipped one hand behind my head, pressing our mouths together in a kiss so deep that it verged on the edge of painful. I yelped as he nibbled my lower lip and then moaned against his mouth, losing any will or desire to resist him further. Whatever he wished to do with me…tonight, I would let him.

His knee nudged my legs open, and I happily let them spread apart, trembling as he cupped a hand between them.

He let out one long, shaky breath and paused, resting his forehead on mine. "I couldna want ye more, lass."

He kissed me and crawled off, leaving me wanting and confused. "Then, have me." The words sounded ridiculous, even to me, but I wanted nothing more.

"No. If I had ye now, I would no be able to let ye leave, and ye have said that ye must."

Chapter 24

"I know it seems like you've got a big decision to make, but can I let you in on a secret?"

I sat with my legs dangling in the castle's pond, leaning back on my hands as I watched Cooper making a mud pie along its shore. I turned to hold out a hand to help Mitsy who was lifting the bottom of her dress so that she could join me.

"Sure, shoot." Mitsy kicked off her shoes and allowed her feet to sink into the water, sighing as it soothed her pregnancy-swollen feet. I could remember exactly how she felt.

"Oh, that's nice. That's really nice." The bottom hem of her dress dropped into the water and she cursed, "Damn these dresses. Usually they're not that bad, but now I just want to live in a pair of yoga pants until this baby decides to drop out of me."

I laughed, patting her arm in sympathy. "I understand."

She waved a hand in dismissal. "Anyhow, back to what I was saying. Don't battle it."

"I'm sorry. I don't know what you mean."

Mitsy wasn't the type of person I would have pegged as being intuitive. I liked her immensely, but it surprised me that she'd been able to so easily figure out what I stewed over.

"Was it so easy for you? Deciding to stay here?"

"Yes. Not right away, I guess. But as soon as I realized that everyone that I loved was here, there was nothing else left for me back home. Modern conveniences meant nothing compared to all of that."

"I do have people that I love who aren't here. Jeffrey, Cooper, Bebop." She didn't realize that it wasn't a battle over whether to stay or go. I knew I couldn't stay here. I simply fought a war with myself trying to accept that.

"I don't know who Bebop is, but Jeffrey and Cooper are

right here with you and, as far as I can see, they look very happy."

They did, but we'd only been here a few days. How would Cooper feel in a few months when he couldn't go out and buy any more dinosaur toys? What kind of mood would Jeffrey be in come football season when there was no television for him to watch it on?

"Sure, but that's because neither one of them expects to stay here."

"How do you know that? Jeffrey would do anything for you. I've only known the man a few days, and I can see that."

I shrugged. That was precisely the problem. Jeffrey's whole life had been a series of sacrifices he'd made for me. I couldn't ask him for anything else. I wouldn't. "Believe me, I know that if I asked Jeffrey to do so, he would. It's the very reason I will never ask it of him."

"Let me ask you something." Mitsy was incredibly direct.

I appreciated it. Her honesty was refreshing, and it made it impossible to feel like a stranger in her presence.

"If you weren't worried about Cooper and Jeffrey, would you stay? At least for a while?"

I nodded but then caught myself. "Yes. I mean, if Eoghanan wanted me to, but he's not asked me. Not directly."

Mitsy laughed, "Eoghanan wouldn't. As far as men go, he's one of the best communicators I've ever seen. He's thoughtful, attentive, but he's incredibly self-sacrificing. He would never ask anything if he thought it selfish. Did he not tell you anything about what happened to him?"

"Not much more than what you mentioned the other day."

"I know, I was vague on purpose. I didn't want to go into the whole story in front of him. Eoghanan would have tried to downplay it, and his actions were too noteworthy for that."

"What happened?" I lifted my weight off of my arms, stretching and twisting my wrists so that I could settle in to finally hear the story I'd been waiting for.

BETHANY CLAIRE

"Baodan was married to someone before me. Her name was Osla, and she died very early on in their marriage. That was over seven years ago and, from the time of her death until right before Eoghanan's injury, Baodan believed Eoghanan responsible."

"Why?" It was a notion almost more difficult for me to believe than learning that witches and time travel existed.

"Baodan and Eoghanan had another brother, Niall, a lousy scumbag who manipulated everyone in their family for years…"

She continued, explaining what Eoghanan had done for Osla during her life and then for Baodan after her death, sacrificing his relationship with his brother to keep from hurting him. Then, how he'd saved Mitsy by stepping in front of Niall's blade, protecting both her and her unborn child.

"He's the rarest of men, Grace. He will do anything for the people he loves, even let them go if he thinks that's what they need. He would never ask you to stay, but it will break his heart if you leave. Nobody else is going to tell you that, but I will. He loves you, even if he doesn't know that yet; even if he hasn't said it to you, he does. And you love him, no matter the length of time that you've known him. Morna would not have sent you here otherwise. Believe me. She's that good."

I watched as she pulled her feet out of the water and stood, readying herself to take her leave.

"And you know what else? She wouldn't have let Cooper and Jeffrey wind up back here unless they were meant to be here as well. Just something to think about. I'll catch you later." She started the short walk back to the castle. "I have to pee again. I have to pee all the time now. Literally, like twenty times a day."

* * *

"Hey, Coop. Can I sit with ya a minute?"
Cooper smiled, nodded as his head still faced the pond. It

was his dad's voice; he'd know it anywhere. "'Course you can. You know you don't have to ask me. You're the dad, ya know?"

"I know, but sometimes a man needs his space. I didn't want to interrupt you if you needed some thinkin' time."

A man...he liked the way that sounded. He wasn't a man yet, but as soon as he lost all of his baby teeth, he would be. Only a few more years to go. "No, I wasn't thinkin.' I was just watching the sky and," he held up his muddy fingers, "making this mud pie. I do my thinking in the mornings."

"Right. My early bird. What have you been thinking lately?"

Cooper took a breath, trying to remember everything. He thought about so many things, surely his dad didn't expect him to list each one. "About what?"

"About this place? What do you think about it? Are you ready to go home soon?"

Home? Out of all the things that he'd thought about, home wasn't one of them. He liked it here too much to think about home. "No, I'm not ready to go home, Dad. We don't have to right away, do we?"

His dad rubbed his back a little. "No son, I was just seeing if you were homesick."

"I only get homesick when I'm not with you and Mom." That wasn't completely true. "And when I don't have my bag of dinosaurs, but guess what, Dad?"

"What?"

"Bao...Baoghan...Baodan. Umm...I think I'm gonna have to come up with a nickname for him too – like I did E-o. Anyway, that guy," he pointed in the direction of the castle so his dad would know who he was talking about, "he brought me my bag this morning. He said it just appeared on the doorstep. I guess that old witch sent it back for me. So now I won't ever be homesick. I have everything I need." Everything he needed not to be homesick, but he still missed one thing. "What about you, Dad? Are you homesick?"

Dad scooted closer to him, pulling him into his lap. "Nope. I'm the same way. As long as I'm with you and your mother, I'm all set. There's only one thing that would make it extra cool."

Cooper knew right away what his dad was talking about, and he nodded. "Bebop."

"Yep. Bebop would love it here."

"Yeah, he would. Dad, do you think we could get Bebop here? That way we wouldn't ever have to leave?"

"I don't know, Coop. Maybe. But that is sort of what I wanted to talk to you about. Do you see your Mom over there?"

Of course he saw her. He'd been watching her sad face all day. She didn't want to leave here either. "Yeah, she's sad. She doesn't want to leave E-o, but she feels like she has to. For us."

Dad kissed him on his head, messing with his hair, bouncing around his curls. "You are such a smart kid, Coop."

"If I don't want to leave, and you don't want to leave, then Mom doesn't need to feel like she has to either. We could all just stay."

Dad stood suddenly, smiling down at him. "My thoughts exactly, Coop. My thoughts exactly."

Chapter 25

Dinner consisted of a meaty and delicious stew served with a loaf of bread that, while tasty, was hard enough to serve as a weapon should the need arise. I'd hoped to retire early, not to sleep, but just to seek some time alone. I seemed to be needing a lot of that lately—to think and perhaps sulk a while. It didn't happen.

I'd gotten half a dozen steps out of the dining hall before Kenna McMillan stopped me. Eoghanan's mother was a stunning woman who showed only the slightest signs of aging with a few perfectly-placed strands of hair turning gray. On her, it was rather fetching.

She was also one of the most kind and open-minded women I'd ever met. Mitsy's blunt way of speaking and no-nonsense attitude came as no surprise, she'd been born in the twenty-first century, after all, but Kenna rivaled her.

I'd expected a woman born so many centuries earlier, in a time when women were often thought of in a very different way, to be more reserved in her speech, more judgmental perhaps of situations that differed from societal expectations. She was none of these things.

She'd opened her son's home and her arms to my family, never questioning the odd situation, never making us feel unwelcome or "less-than". She said exactly what she thought and took bull from no one. I hoped that if I spent more time around her and Mitsy some of that attitude might rub off on me.

"Grace, do ye have a moment?"

I slowed my pace, allowing her to catch up to me. She quickly looped an arm with mine and deftly steered me in the opposite direction of where I'd been heading. "I verra much wish that…what is it that Mitsy has called it? Email? I wish the invention of such a thing could arise now and no hundreds of years after I'm dead."

I laughed, patting her hand sympathetically as she walked me out the back door of the castle and into the garden. "News travel too slow for you? I have to admit, I'm enjoying the break from it all. It's nice not to be so connected, to know that people can't reach you every second of every day."

Kenna nodded. "Aye, I wouldna want to be that available perhaps, but I can see how it would be verra helpful when guests are arriving. They could send news of their arrival more than just the morning before."

"Are you expecting guests?"

"Aye, the Conalls are coming to stay with us until the arrival of Mitsy's babe. They sent a messenger some three days before they were to arrive here, but the man fell ill and only just arrived today."

"Oh. Well, what can I help you with?"

She shook her head, laughing, "Oh, no a thing, dear. 'Tis only that the bedchamber that ye are staying in…I'm afraid we willna have enough rooms for everyone if ye stay in it alone."

"Oh." For a moment, I wondered if she meant to ask us to leave, but she quickly continued to clarify.

"Now, doona think I'm giving ye an opportunity to slip away from here, for no one of us wants that. 'Tis only we must find some other room to place ye."

I took a deep breath, relaxing the sudden anxiety that had built up. I was glad she wasn't ready for me to leave. I wasn't ready to either, no matter how much I knew I needed to.

"I'll just stay with Cooper and Jeffrey. It will be no problem. I can sleep on the floor, or Jeffrey can."

Kenna regarded me as if I'd just suggested we run the length of the garden completely naked. "Sleep on the floor? No. I'll enter me grave before I have a guest in me," she corrected herself, "me son's home, sleep on the floor."

She made the correction because technically it was

correct, but I didn't believe for a second that she was any less hands-on in the running of the castle than she was before her husband's death. Mitsy had mentioned to me, when she'd told me Eoghanan's story, how Kenna had been so ill for so long, reduced nearly to death. Standing before this strong, beautiful, headstrong woman now, I couldn't begin to picture it.

"Well," I started. "I'm sure this isn't customary, but I don't think Mitsy would mind. I could stay with Mitsy and..." I felt incredibly uncomfortable making a suggestion about how things should be done, but it seemed as if she wanted my help in finding a solution. "Baodan could move in with Eoghanan for a few nights."

She stopped walking and faced me, gathering up both of my hands in hers. "No, that wouldna be customary. Neither is what I am going to suggest, but it seems I will have to help ye on, since ye willna make the suggestion yerself. I willna ask me son to spend the night without his pregnant wife, nor she without him."

She fumbled with my hands a bit, hesitating. I could tell the exact moment she decided to get on with what she meant to say. She straightened, looked me straight in the eyes, and the corner of her mouth pulled up a bit into a knowing smile.

"Ye will stay with Eoghanan."

My eyes widened. She laughed before I could respond, releasing her grip on my hands and walking hastily back into the castle before I could argue, leaving me standing alone in the garden with my mouth hanging slightly open.

She was a modern woman indeed. If there'd ever been a woman born out of her true time, it was Kenna McMillan.

* * *

"What are you doing, Grace?"

I messed around the bedchamber I'd been placed in, doing my best to waste as much time as possible before I went to invite myself into Eoghanan's room. I'd been pretending to

133

tidy things up, but the room was immaculate so I suspected I looked a bit mad, flittering about the room, lifting objects as I brushed away at nothing with my hand. Jeffrey's question confirmed my suspicions.

"Uh, hey, I was just…" I gave up. "I don't know what I'm doing. What's up?"

He smiled and stepped inside, moving to place an arm around me, pulling me in close.

"Who would have thought, huh? All of this," he motioned to the room with his free hand. "It's crazy, but kind of wonderful too. Coop really loves it here."

I nodded, gladly leaning into Jeffrey's comforting arm. "Yes, I'm sure he does for a few days, but he'll be ready to get home soon."

"I wouldn't be so sure, Grace. He's an odd kid; I kind of think this place suits him even better than back home."

I couldn't imagine what he was getting at, but I wished he'd stop. Believing that there was a possibility that Cooper could be happy here made me hope for something I couldn't have. "Well, there's a lot more to it than just Cooper's happiness."

Jeffrey squeezed my shoulder and kissed the side of my temple, rubbing my back sympathetically. "Are you saying that you wouldn't be happy here?"

I shook my head against his chest. "No. I think I would."

"So what's there to think about, Grace? Let's stay. What have you got to lose? It's not a prison here. Mitsy and Baodan have both said that should you ever want to leave, should you ever need to return home, Morna would help you." He released me and paced around the room. "If you leave now though, you'll regret it, Grace. You'll wonder forever if you missed out on the real thing. The thing you're never gonna get from me, the thing you want Cooper to see exists."

Of course he would give me permission to stay. I'd expect nothing less from him, which is why I'd hoped he wouldn't realize how much I wanted to stay. I'd been a fool to think I could hide anything from him.

"Jeffrey, you don't want to be here. Are you saying that you'll leave? Because you won't, I know you wouldn't leave Cooper here, and I am not going to ask you to do that for me."

"You're not asking me, Grace. I'm telling you that I like it here, too. I'd like it anywhere as long as I have you and Cooper."

"No, we're not going to sacrifice Cooper's childhood, your job, your life, just because of this." I didn't even know what 'this' was. "This thing with Eoghanan."

"His childhood?" Jeffrey's voice was quickly growing frustrated. "A childhood of what? Seeing his mother unhappy because she sacrificed what she really wanted to give him what she *thought* he needed. A childhood of being picked on because he's smarter than all the other kids in his class and he'd rather read a book than play a videogame?"

Jeffrey had made his point. I was using Cooper as an excuse. "Fine." Tears started to fill my eyes, and my voice cracked as I spoke. "It's not about Cooper. It's about you and how guilty I feel that every decision in your life has been about me. And…it's about Eoghanan. What if he doesn't even want me?"

He stormed past me, stopping in the doorway. "What a load of shit, Grace. The man wouldn't spend half his days writing about you if he didn't want you. You're scared, and you need to grow up. You can only use being a mother as an excuse not to have your own life for so long."

The shock on my face must have been evident, for he nodded, continuing. "That's right, Grace. The man is crazy about you. I was playing with Cooper last night, and we stumbled across some old room where he writes. You should see it, Grace. Only a total idiot would turn down someone that thinks that highly of them. There are few men that could ever be worthy of you as far as I'm concerned, but he's one of them. Do not be an idiot."

He stepped out into the hallway.

"And you know what? My mind is made up anyway. Even if you decide to leave, I'm staying right here."

Chapter 26

The room took some finding, but shortly after Jeffrey left me, I went in search of it.

The room was filled with books all neatly organized amongst cleanly-kept shelves, candles ready to be lit lining the room.

I moved slowly, setting it alight, taking in the beautiful cave-like atmosphere. It would have been a nice place to work on my article, which now would remain eternally unfinished.

Jeffrey didn't make idle threats or promises. If he said he'd made up his mind to stay, he would stay. And so would I.

In the center of the room was a large table, and right in the center lay the open-faced journal. Eoghanan must have truly thought the room hidden to have left it out so blatantly. It was wrong of me to be here, to delve into his private thoughts without permission, but curiosity overwhelmed me. I truly had no right to shame Cooper for eavesdropping. He came by it honestly.

The journal was new, not only the entries, but the binding itself was modern. It was the sort of special journal I could've ordered from a craftsman; the outside leather, the pages made of the highest quality paper, all sewn in thick gold-colored threads. It had the look of something old, but the date embossed on the inside flap of leather showed the date of its creation—two thousand and fourteen. I imagined it had arrived at the doorstep via Morna, right alongside my son's dinosaurs.

I thumbed the pages for a bit, running my fingers over the ink-dried pages, without really looking at the words, trying to work up the nerve to actually read them. When I finally did, I found myself taken aback. He'd not written so much about me, as for me.

"Do ye remember the day ye spent with Cooper in the park? I only know the lad's name for 'tis what ye called him when ye spoke. Ye have the loveliest voice I've ever heard."

I could think of few things less lovely than the sound of my voice. I cringed every time I heard it on any sort of home movie or recording.

"If ye ever read this, 'twill be many moons from now, but for me, 'twas just this afternoon. Me body is bleeding and wounded from the journey, and I write with pages so far from me eyes I canna see them, but I must write every piece of ye down lest I forget ye. 'Twould break me heart to no remember every instant that I saw."

I put a finger on the page to hold my place and skipped forward a handful of pages, smiling as I did so. He'd told the truth about the page being far from his eyes. The page I read now was scribbled messily, the lines and words crooked with the effort it took him to hold the pen and move his fingers.

As his shoulder slowly healed, so did the neatness of his handwriting. It came as no surprise that in full form with the full movement of his shoulder restored that his last entry showed handwriting that was shockingly straight and neat.

I returned back to where I'd left off reading.

"I have no ever been so frightened in me life as when I woke inside the park. The tall stone structures and the deafening noise were enough to make a man mad. Me head and heart pounded as I struggled to understand the sights around me, and then me eyes found ye and the wee lad. Yer long blonde hair blew with the breeze, and ye laughed as ye pushed the boy on a strange seat that sent him flying in the air. Ye

wore the breeches of a man, though I've never seen a man wear something so tight. God help me, lass, I couldna keep me eyes off yer bum. I couldna believe when I looked around and saw many lassies dressed such. 'Tis no wonder Morna says there are numbers of more people in the world now than in me own time. I imagine men have a verra hard time getting much work done. Ye wore such lovely colors, the greens and blues in yer top making yer eyes sparkle in the sun. I doona even know yer name, but me only dream tonight, should sleep find me, is that I should get to see yer face once again."

I closed my eyes as I reached the end of the entry, my fingers lingering lovingly on the last line. I remembered so little about that day. To have him detail it so attentively was as if he'd started caring for me the first day he'd ever seen me. The adoration in his words was overwhelming. I flipped forward, finding an entry dated the day Cooper and I arrived at the inn.

"God, me heart stopped beating when I saw ye standing in the kitchen. To see ye when ye canna see me is one thing; to know that ye are looking back at me is another. I have no ever felt such a way before, lass. There is something between us, aye? I know that we doona know each other, but 'tis there; a feeling that tells me I canna go back to a life before I met ye. I think 'tis how it should be, perhaps. I wouldna know, 'tis a verra new experience for me. I knew there was a reason me travels back sent me to ye. I dinna believe Morna when she said 'twas no her doing. It was, and I couldna be more grateful for it. I am verra fond of ye, lass. I

139

think in time, ye will be of me as well."

I'd been too shocked at Cooper's exclamations of knowing the man to let it sink in at the time, but I'd felt much the same way. A sudden shift in my being, like a gear in my brain clicking into place when I saw him. From that moment, I couldn't be in the same room with him without being intensely aware of him every moment, without feeling his presence deep in my bones.

> *"I knew the wee lad had seen me, but I'd hoped it hadna been so clearly that he'd recognize me. I hope that the idea dinna scare ye, lass. I saw yer eyes widen at Cooper's exclamation and aye, I suppose 'tis a bit unsettling to think that I might have been watching ye without yer knowledge. And although I have, 'tis been nothing but care and admiration in me heart while doin so."*

I had no doubt about that. As he'd said, Morna controlled where he went, not him. Cooper had known that as well; from his first glimpse of him in the airport, when he'd tried to tell me about him and I'd been frightened, he'd said he could see what a good man he was from his eyes.

There were several more entries that I skimmed, coming finally to the last one, written only this morning.

> *"I am a man who has denied meself many things, but none has been so difficult as denying meself ye. To know that ye plan to leave here 'tis no something I wish to think about. I understand why ye feel that ye must, but ye are wrong. Ye belong here. Ye and Cooper and Jeffrey; ye could all be a part of this family. I need ye. I love ye, lass. Doona leave."*

Mitsy was right. He cared too much about others and too

little about himself to ask me what he wanted anywhere but in these journals. What a gift, though he'd not wished for me to see it, to know how he felt; to know that he'd not slowly warmed to me, but opened his heart to me so immediately, trusting that some things are meant to be so much more readily than I had.

I closed the journal, my eyes brimming with tears and abundant gratitude for this strange, miraculous change in the path of my life.

I heard sudden footsteps behind me. I knew it was Eoghanan even before I turned.

"I've been looking everywhere for ye, lass.

Chapter 27

"I'm sorry. I shouldn't have…" I trailed off as I stood and faced him, waiting for him to approach me. Truthfully, I was much more sorry that I'd been caught than having read the journal.

When he reached me, he cupped either side of my face, brushing away a loose tear with his thumb, before kissing me gently. I relaxed against him, matching his slow kisses with my own.

After a moment, he pulled away, leaning in to whisper in my ear. "Doona be sorry. They were meant for ye, only mayhap no so soon."

I wound one of my hands into his hair, holding him close to me as I spoke. "It's not too soon. I'm not going anywhere. You can thank Jeffrey for helping me see that I couldn't."

"Aye, I shall thank him, lass, but no tonight." He kissed me again, but not slowly like before; it was deeper, more urgent and I molded my body against him, my knees growing weak with anticipation.

A sudden commotion sounded below us, the voices of many people echoing up through the stairwell. I groaned internally, pulling away from his kiss and allowing my head to drop disappointingly onto his shoulder. "Your guests are here."

"Guests?" He lifted my head, asking for more explanation.

"Yes, the Conalls are here, I think. They've come to stay until the baby is born."

He nodded. "I am no surprised." Gripping my hand, he pulled me out of the room and started moving down the stairwell rather quickly.

I assumed he was taking me to greet them, but as he turned the corner leading to his bedchamber rather than continuing to the great hall, I smiled. "Where are we going?"

"To bed, Grace. Ye can meet them in the morning. It nearly killed me to no bury meself inside ye before. I willna be interrupted now."

If we'd not been moving, I knew my knees would have actually buckled. I'd always thought that a dramatic cliché, but it wasn't. His words thrilled me so much that my heart sped up to a frightening pace. I could scarcely breathe. All of the blood seemed to drain from my brain, leaving no other thoughts but him and what I wanted him to do to me.

* * *

He'd been a fool to let her leave his bed the evening before without begging her to stay. He was finished behaving as a fool.

It was the part of himself he hated most—his desire to always do what he thought right. In that moment of cowardice, he'd believed it right of him to let her leave if she thought it best. But he'd realized his mistake the moment he'd left his room. There was nothing right about Grace leaving his life.

How many times had his notions of right or wrong been misguided? All that had happened with Osla, Niall, and Baodan should have shown him that. Sometimes he made very bad mistakes. Letting her believe he didn't want her here, even for a moment, was one of them.

He needed her, unlike anyone he'd ever met. He needed her and Cooper to show him that he could be the man he knew he was, not the man others had believed him to be for so many years.

She needed him as well.

Eoghanan knew that he could help her open up to believing that being a mother didn't negate her need to be desired or loved. Each time he kissed her, he could sense her restraint. Even now as he flung his bedchamber door open, pushing her up against the doorway as he cupped her breast

143

with his hand, she moaned and pushed herself into it. He could feel the effort she put into trying to keep herself from enjoying it fully. Too many years alone had somehow convinced the lass that after motherhood one couldn't express sexual desires. It was the one foolish notion he'd seen in her.

Mothers who were regularly tupped by a man who loved them made the happiest moms; just as dads who found release in their wives were the happiest of men.

He would prove that to her tonight.

* * *

Each flick of his tongue down my neck, each squeeze of my breast through the fabric of my dress had me writhing against him, one part of me desperate for him to undress me, the other part guilty for being so self-indulgent.

As far as I could see, motherhood was the greatest blessing one could receive in life, but with it came a sort of constant, eternal sense of guilt I'd yet to learn how to shake. I'd spent much of my childhood alone under the care of nannies or Jeffrey's father, and I remembered wondering why my parents didn't want to spend time with me. What was so important that they were always gone?

I didn't ever want Cooper to wonder where I was, to ever question whether I thought something else was more important than him. I'd not been able to take a yoga class or get a massage since his birth without feeling guilty for leaving him.

Eoghanan must have sensed my hesitation for he stopped kissing me. Although he kept our bodies pressed together, my back still against the wall, he cupped my head in his hands and spoke. "Where are ye lass? For 'tis no right here with me."

I closed my eyes in resignation of how right he was. I wanted nothing more than to be present, in this moment, to enjoy him in every imaginable way, but something resisted. "Coop, he…"

Eoghanan didn't allow me to finish, covering my mouth

with one of his palms. "Hush, Grace. This night is no about Cooper, nor Jeffrey, nor anyone else within these walls. Ye needn't worry about him. He's with his dad and our new guests, one of whom I know has him up in her lap talking all about his wee dinosaurs. Bri loves children and, even if ye were with Cooper now, she will be the one who has his attention. Tonight..." he released his grip on my mouth and lifted me away from the wall, keeping both hands behind me as he worked at my laces. He spoke in between kisses he placed strategically along my collarbone, "...only ye and me exist in the world. We must help rid the other of the chains we place ourselves in."

He travelled his kisses up the side of my neck, along my jawline as he let go of the laces. He gripped the top of my sleeves and pulled, sending my dress to the floor as he kissed me on the lips once more.

His breathing escalated instantaneously, though I knew he'd yet to glance down at my naked body. His eyes were locked with my own, his voice deep and husky with desire.

"I love ye, Grace. I am no saying it because I want ye in me bed. I say it because I've loved ye since the first time I saw ye. Before ye knew of me existence, I loved ye."

I'd fallen for a similar line once before and wound up with Cooper, but unlike the time before when the man's confession had been laced with beer and delivered simultaneously with the opening of a condom, I felt the truthfulness of Eoghanan's words somewhere deep inside.

It was not the first time I'd felt such a conviction—Eoghanan said nothing he didn't mean. I wouldn't either.

"I won't tell you that part of me doesn't worry that I'm just too caught up in this, that it's foolish of me to say it, because it wouldn't be true. I am worried. I'm scared to death, Eoghanan. I'm scared because I know what you mean. That first time in the kitchen, I felt something too and that seems completely crazy to me." I was rambling but I couldn't stop, my breath coming so rapidly that each intake of air caused my breasts to push against his chest. "Completely crazy. I mean, who does that? Feels this way so fast. It's nuts."

Both of my hands lay on his shoulders, and I found that I was shaking him a bit, and he regarded me with a confused expression.

"I only understood mayhap three words of that, lass. That was a good deal too many words when all I can think about is how much I want to pull those teasing breasts of yers into me mouth. Please say it again, lass, only with less words."

I laughed, leaning in to kiss him gently before moving my lips to his ear. "I only meant, I love you too."

He groaned a deep, delighted sound. In that instant, he lifted me, my legs coming around his waist, his mouth crushing mine as he carried me to his bed. He lay me back gently, rising slowly so that he could stand and look down at me.

I was entirely exposed. I'd not been naked in front of a man since before pregnancy, and my body didn't have the same flawless look it once had. I moved my hands to cover my stomach self-consciously, hoping he wouldn't notice the effort. He did of course.

"Move yer hands, lass."

I kept them in place, shaking my head side to side on the bed. "I'd rather not. It's…"

"I know what they are, Grace. Do ye really think I'm someone that ye should be worried about yer scars with?"

Valid point, but his scar was sort of beautiful. It made him look brave, rugged, and slightly dangerous. I tried to tell him as much. "Yeah, but your scar is sexy. These things…"

Again, he interrupted me, bending to pry my hands off of the flat of my stomach. He kissed the marks, trailing the faded white lines with his lips. "These 'things' as ye call them are reminders of the wonderful lad that ye created, lass. Ye should be proud of them, for they make ye even more beautiful than ye already are."

I surrendered then, allowing him to kiss me at will, any sense of self-consciousness gone. He trailed his kisses lower, nibbling along the inside of my thigh, moving perilously close to the center of my thighs. I couldn't take it, and I squirmed beneath him. I'd gone too long untouched, and if he kissed me there…I wanted to climax with him inside me.

"Eoghanan…take off your clothes."

With his scar no longer tender, he'd been free to don his kilt. He removed it with far too much ease, hardly looking up from his pleasure. I reached down to pull on his hair, hoping he would rise up and meet me.

He crawled slowly over me, nudging my legs apart with his knee before drawing one of my nipples deep into his mouth. I moaned and my hips arched upward, brushing against his erection.

I'd already seen him naked, but to feel him hard and ready against me was enough to make me buck against him in the hopes that he would enter me more quickly.

He smiled up at me knowingly but made no move to hurry himself. Instead, he shifted over me so that he could slip one hand in between my legs while kissing me.

He groaned in response to my readiness. His fingers slipped easily inside me as he sucked on my lower lip, dancing his fingers in and out and over my sensitive nub.

"Eoghanan…I, you have to stop, or I…I'll…" I could hardly form a cohesive sentence.

He delighted in it. "Or ye'll what, lass? 'Tis it no the great pleasure of women that ye may find yer pleasure more than once?"

I simply cried out in response to him, arching my hips into the palm of his hand as I quivered in response to his touch.

"Aye, 'tis, lass, and this night I shall do all I can to help ye find it over and over again."

He kissed me, patiently waiting for my trembles to

subside before pushing me open once again, readying me to accept him. Slowly, he pushed inside me, his breathing escalating with every increasing inch.

"Oh, Grace, I have spent many a night dreaming of what 'twould feel like to be inside ye. No one of me dreams prepared me for this. I could live inside ye."

Chapter 28

We moved together and another climax built quickly within me, and I matched him as he neared the edge of release. When he shuttered within me, I clenched around him, and both of us cried out, my fingernails digging into his shoulders.

"Ach, I knew ye would do that, lass. I doona know why, but I knew it."

I laughed as he relaxed against my shoulder, slowly rolling onto his side.

"I know," I rolled over to face him, my body still humming with aftershocks. "You said something about that the other night."

He grinned, kissing my fingertips that lay loosely between our faces. "Ach, I said many things I no should have."

"Why not?"

"Mayhap 'twas no so much that I shouldn't have said them, only that I would no usually say them."

I nodded, agreeing that was most definitely what it had been, and slowly my eyes started to drift closed. I was happy, and loose, and exhausted. Just as I'd begun to dream, Eohganan wrapped his arms around me and pinched me on the rear.

"Oh no, ye doona get to sleep yet, lass. Do ye no remember what I told ye?"

I opened one eye, leaving the other closed. "What's that?"

"Twice does no equal 'over and over.' I am no done with ye yet."

He had to be kidding. How could he possibly have the energy? "Let's at least take a cat nap first." I scooted in to him, moving my head to his chest and draping one of my legs across him.

"Ye are mad if ye think I'll be able to sleep with ye lying

naked across me." He pulled his head back to look at me. "Grace, what is a 'cat nap'?"

I yawned, stretching into him. "It's an expression, it just means a short nap."

He shook his head, rolling me off him so that he could face me. "A short nap would turn into a long sleep."

"Mmmhmm…" I allowed my eyes to drift closed once again. This time he didn't argue, instead standing to pull back the blankets.

"At least get in the bed, lass."

I did as he asked, rolling to the open part before tucking my legs inside. He joined me, pulling me close to him.

"Thank you," I whispered, planting a kiss on the side of his cheek.

"For what?" He grinned into my lips.

"For not allowing me to talk myself out of this." Voices travelled down the hallway outside his door and I spoke to him, my voice teasing. "See? Everybody is going to bed. It's time to sleep."

"Aye, our guests are being shown to their rooms." He paused, his eyebrows scrunching up in the middle.

"What are you thinking?"

"I'm counting. I doona think we have enough bedchambers."

I smiled, laughing into his chest. "You didn't, but you do now."

"Did ye build us one, Grace? 'Tis a talent I dinna know ye had."

"No. Your mother kicked me out of my room."

"She what?" The covers flew back and he tried to leave the bed, but I jumped up to stop him, grabbing his shoulders and pulling him backward.

"Cool your jets. She assigned me to another room."

"Aye? And whose room is that? I doona think Baodan will make room for ye in his bed." He paused and grinned,

"Actually, he'd be a fool to no allow two women inside it, but his wife would put a stop to that."

I rolled my eyes. It didn't matter what century they were from, men's minds still thought in much the same way. "No. Your mother asked, no instructed, me to sleep in your room."

"No, she dinna?" Eoghanan's eyes widened in disbelief.

"Yes. I promise you she did. I was rather surprised myself."

"Aye, I doona know what to say. I doona think I've ever been so surprised." He laughed a moment before reaching over and pulling me on top of him, pulling my head down to meet his kiss. "Ye wouldna want to disobey me mother, would ye?"

I laughed but remained straddling him, no longer feeling so sleepy. "No, but I think the word she used was "sleep" not…not this." I swept my hand downward to motion to the both of us.

"Oh, we'll sleep lass. 'Til midday if I have anything to say about it, but no just now."

Chapter 29

True to his word, he exhausted me so entirely that I did sleep until midday, only to find myself alone in his room when I woke. He meant it as a courtesy—rising before me so that we would not appear before the new guests at exactly the same time, coming from exactly the same direction. I'd been worried about it all night, so I relaxed upon finding myself alone.

I would be able to greet the Conalls without it being quite so apparent what Eoghanan and I had been up to all night, although if their rooms were close, I had no doubt some of them knew well enough.

"Mom! Hey, which room are you in, Mom?"

The little voice sent my heart pattering a million miles a minute, and I leapt from the bed in a panic looking for my dress so that I could slip it on before Cooper burst through the door. I managed it with not a second to spare, reaching for the handle just as the door flung open.

"There you are, Mom! You missed breakfast by a long shot. Dad said you were around here somewhere." He peeked his head inside. "Isn't this E-o's room?"

I was suddenly very warm. "Umm…yeah, with all of the new people in the castle, I had to give my room up for their guests."

He shrugged. "Oh, okay, cool. Did you sleep on the floor or something?"

I nodded, leaning down to pick him up. "Yeah, something like that." It wasn't a complete lie…we had been on the floor for part of the night.

"Maybe tonight you should ask E-o if you can switch places. You get the floor and he gets the bed. That would be only fair. I bet he'd let you."

I laughed, kissing his temple as I walked out of the room with him still on my hip. God bless the innocent minds of children. "Yeah, I'll be sure to ask him."

"Hey, guess what, Mom?"

"What, Coop?"

"There's even more people coming! Ba-o, that's my new name for Mitsy's husband, and this other guy Donal, just told everyone. They said like a bunch of clans or something. I don't know what a clan is, but it sounds like a lot of people are coming to stay here for a gathering."

He really emphasized the word 'gathering.' It had clearly been spoken of as if it were something very special.

"Oh yeah?"

"Yeah, I bet it's going to be tons of fun."

It was a reasonable thought for a child to have, and I imagined the men who had decided on such a gathering thought very much the same thing.

As for the women, I could all but hear the internal groan of every woman in the castle, thinking that instead of "tons of fun," it was going to be tons of work.

* * *

Cooper and I were greeted at the bottom of the stairs by Jeffrey, who smiled knowingly and much too wide at the sight of me.

"Hey Coop, I think Lady McMillan has a job for you if you're willing to help."

He immediately squirmed out of my arms. "Yeah, yeah, where is she?"

Jeffrey pointed in the direction of the kitchens. "I think she's in that direction."

"I bet I can find her. I think I'm gonna make a nickname for her too. Lady Mac, I think."

At the same time that Jeffrey shook his head, I said. "Uh, no Coop. Sorry, some people don't need nicknames."

"Oh, come on. I bet she'd like it."

I'm sure he was right. Still, it was too casual a name.

"No. I agree with your mother. You call her Lady McMillan. Understand?" Jeffrey stepped in to end the conversation.

"Yes, sir." His face drooped for just a second but he lifted it quickly, smiling and shrugging his shoulders before he took off in her direction. "It was worth a shot, huh?"

Jeffrey and I laughed in unison as we watched him leave. As soon as he was out of earshot, Jeffrey turned to me, that same creepy grin on his face. "Good on you, Gracie."

I held up both hands in question to him. "What's with this 'good on you' stuff? Are you British or something? I'm pretty sure that's like a UK thing. And don't call me Gracie."

He laughed. "Hmm...I don't know, maybe it is. I've watched a lot of BBC in my day. Still, you get my drift. You clearly had fun last night."

"Why would you say that? There's no way you can tell anything by looking at me."

"Oh yes. Yes I can. You have circles under your eyes, which means that you didn't sleep, but your cheeks are rosy and your skin is all aglow which means you didn't mind it."

"That's quite the scientific observation."

"It is. I'm an expert."

"Pffhh..." I made the sound as I shook my head at him, ready to change the conversation. "So where is everybody? I guess it's time I show myself."

"They're all outside. You'll like them. Cool bunch. So...after last night...I guess that means we're staying?"

We started walking toward the outside doors together, and I turned my head to regard him skeptically. "I thought you were staying regardless?"

He smiled. "Forgive me, I am. I just misspoke. I meant to say, 'I guess that means you're staying?'"

"Yes, I'm staying."

"Good."

Just as we reached them, the grand doors of the castle swung open. Immediately, Mitsy latched onto me, sweeping me into the crowd, introducing me rather excitedly.

"There you are, Grace." She held onto my arm but extended her neck to call after a group of women standing near the pond. "Bri, Blaire, Adelle, come meet Grace!" Three women, two of which I could have sworn were twins, all smiling, made their way to me. "This is Bri," she pointed to the first woman bouncing a baby on her hip. "This is Blaire," she pointed to the second woman. "I know they look like sisters, but they're not; although, most people think they are. Long story, Eoghanan can tell you sometime. And this," she pointed to the last woman, "is Adelle, Bri's mother."

I smiled, shaking all of their hands. "Nice to meet you."

Mitsy allowed them no chance to respond, quickly yanking me toward another group of people, and so the routine continued until I had been introduced to everyone in their party.

"You're glad to have some people about, aren't you?"

Mitsy laughed, releasing her grip on me for the first time. "Yes. Sorry. The Conalls...we're all family, and Bri and I have been best friends a long time. I'm just happy for all of us to be in the same place. Plus...I'm glad to have some extra hands to help with this sudden gathering."

"Understandably so. I'll be happy to help in any way that you need me to."

"Thank you. And now..." she pointed in Eoghanan's direction, "I'll release you for a while."

She flittered away quickly, and I made my way over to Eoghanan who, much to my surprise, gathered me up in his arms and kissed me rather thoroughly.

"Well, good morning to you, too." I laced my fingers with his as he led me away from the crowd, back inside the castle.

"Aye, 'tis a wonderful morning. Though, I'm afraid I've

some unfortunate news."

Dread settled immediately in my gut. "What?"

He twirled a strand of my hair. "Doona look so worried, lass. 'Tis nothing all that bad. I'll be away tomorrow—down to the village to fetch supplies for the gathering. I expect the lassies will need yer help here."

"Oh, I don't mind helping. I already told Mitsy I'd do whatever they need me to."

"Aye, ye say that now, but ye doona yet know all the women who will be leading the charge around here tomorrow. No only me mother, but also Rhona, our head maid and a lifelong resident of this castle. And if I know the Conalls, their Mary will be anxious to take charge of something. And they'll need her help, I'm no saying that, 'tis only that if Mary helps, then Adelle will jump in just to aggravate her."

"Sounds like you've been around them a lot."

He shook his head. "No all that much truthfully, but it doesna take verra long to see how a group of headstrong women behave when ye put them all to task on the same thing. 'Tis a powerful but frightening force."

Chapter 30

"I am pleased to see ye doing so well, cousin. The blade wound was such that only one with Morna's powers could heal it."

Eoghanan rode next to Eoin Conall, his cousin on his mother's side, and shuddered thinking back on that night. Death had meant little to him then, but now he had much more to lose. The knowledge that death had been so close to him only a few months prior still made him uneasy. He couldn't imagine never having had the chance to know Grace or her bonny son.

"Aye, I am verra glad as well. I owe the witch a great debt."

"I doubt Morna sees it that way."

Eoghanan nodded. "I know that she doesna, but it makes me feel no less indebted."

"Whoa, buddy! Whoa….Whoa…are you trying to make me fall off you? 'Cause you're doing a good job."

Cooper's voice from a short distance in front of him caught Eoghanan's attention. Giving his own horse a nudge, Eoghanan rode to catch up with him. When Cooper had insisted on having his own horse, they'd given him the oldest, gentlest beast in their stables. The horse was doing nothing to dismount Cooper, barely moving at a slow trot.

Still, Cooper had both arms wrapped around his horse's neck, his little chest pressed flat against the horse's mane.

"Have ye no ever ridden a horse before, Cooper?"

The child lifted his head just slightly, still maintaining his tight grip on the creature's neck.

"Of course, I haven't. I'm a city boy. Born and raised in

NYC. The only horses I've ever seen were pulling those buggy things for tourists."

Eoghanan didn't know half of what the lad meant, but he believed that he'd not seen many horses. "Would ye like to ride with me, lad?"

"No. I gotta learn if I'm gonna live here, don't I?"

It pleased Eoghanan to no end that Cooper knew his parents planned to stay here. It made it seem more certain, more real. "Aye, ye will need to learn, but it doesna have to be today if ye doona wish it. I can teach ye back at the castle, when there are no so many others around."

Cooper shook his head, determined to keep going. "No, I don't care if they watch. It'll just take me a little time to get used to it."

"I admire yer stubbornness, Cooper. Look," he pointed to the edge of the village in front of them. "We are almost there. I'll ride beside ye to the village edge, where we will dismount and tie up our horses."

"Okay," Cooper lifted his chest, testing out his balance now that someone was there to aid in the case of a fall. "If you insist."

* * *

The young witch Jinty watched with disbelieving eyes at the group of men approaching the village. She remained shaded amongst the trees. The men wouldn't know who she was or what role she'd played in the destruction of their family. Still, better not to be seen.

She wasn't interested in the Conalls, she knew them well enough—the tall dark headed Scot and the blonde one, both formidable as always, but utterly unimportant to her. The young boy she'd never seen before. There was only one that caught her attention, only one that sent rage rushing through her very fingertips, morphing into hatred as it settled inside her heart.

Eoghanan, the red-headed demon who'd taken from her the one man who could have delivered her from a life of solitude. She'd thought him dead. No one had seen the bastard McMillan brother in many moons. Clearly death had reached for him, the scar running the length of his body showed her that much, but he'd survived. Perhaps death was too much a kindness for him. He deserved to be subjected to the same lonely life he'd forced her to live.

When her beloved, Niall McMillan, had come to her the first time she'd been a young girl lost—left alone after the death of her grandmother, forced to survive with only her powers and the knowledge of herbs her grandmother had left her with. He'd given her a purpose and his heart.

One task in exchange for a life spent together—to help him gain his place as Laird. Years she'd worked for him, dutifully producing poisons, never asking questions, waiting for him to come to her, only accepting his love when he offered it.

They'd come so close to victory. Then Eoghanan had turned Baodan against Niall, and her beloved had met his death. No matter who ran the blade through him, Eoghanan was to blame. Once again, she was alone in the world—the witch in the woods, shunned until one wished bad fortune to fall upon another.

Soon, that bad fortune would reach Eoghanan. She would make sure he was as lonely as she.

She watched the group of men closely, following a short distance behind them as they made their way through the village, stopping to gather men and supplies. There would be a gathering at the castle and all were invited. It would be the perfect time to act against him, but first she needed to find his greatest weakness, the thing he loved most in the world, and rip it from him.

It would be a difficult job. The mysterious McMillan brother had no family of his own, no one had ever seen him in

159

the company of a lass. But everyone cared about something. Jinty would find it in time.

Infectious laughter drifted from the direction she watched, and Jinty's eye's rested on the child once again. Eoghanan had the boy in his arms, and the look in his eyes was unmistakable. He cared for the child.

She couldn't imagine why or what role this young boy now played in Eoghanan's life, but there was no denying that he adored the child. He watched over him with cautious eyes, stood near him at all times. Whatever the reason, today the child was in his charge.

There was still much she would have to learn, but the gathering would be the perfect place to do so. If the child was now a permanent fixture in Eoghanan's life, she could think of no greater revenge than to change that for him.

Chapter 31

As Eoghanan predicted, there was plenty of chaos the next morning as the group of women—Mitsy, Kenna, Rhona, Mary, Adelle, Bri, Blaire, and myself—tried to direct everyone to specific tasks for the day. However, after a few hours of disagreements and power struggles, we all fell into a nice routine, each of us setting to our tasks with a dogged determination to have our jobs completed before the men returned.

I'd been paired with Mitsy for the day and found myself with the very easy and enjoyable task of overseeing Jeffrey, Adelle's husband, Hew, and a handful of other men as they set up tents for the other arriving guests.

"Are you sure I'm not needed anywhere else? I feel a bit guilty, watching these guys work when all of the other women are busy working inside."

Mitsy placed a hand on my arm to keep me from getting up. "I am absolutely sure. Believe me. Kenna, Rhona, Adelle, and Mary each have control over a quarter of the castle, which is just how they like it. They feel like they're playing boss, but they won't be in each other's way. Bri is busy with baby Ellie, and I'm too hot and pregnant to do much of anything. And I don't want to be alone, so that's where you come in."

"Okay, but are you sure you don't want to hang with Bri and the baby? I could help with the work that way."

"No," she said the word quite urgently.

I realized that her impending motherhood had her scared to death. She didn't want to be around babies just yet. I understood completely. I'd been much the same way.

"Okay, I'll stay. It will all be alright, you know?" I relaxed, leaning back against the side of the castle, realizing that it was rather foolish to argue myself into more work. "It's scary, especially when you didn't grow up dreaming of being a mother." She looked surprised that I would infer this about her. "I didn't either, but I promise, you just take it one day at a time. It will be the best thing that ever happens to you."

Her lip suddenly quivered, and I reached out to rub her shoulder, understanding all too well the swell of emotions pregnancy hormones could bring.

"I know that…it's just…gosh, I look at Bri and she was born for this. I wasn't." Her chest started to shake as she struggled to hold back tears.

"Oh, Misty. That child…" I pointed to her belly, recreating the very words that Jeffery's father had said to me once, during my pregnancy with Cooper, "you were handpicked to be its mother. There's no one else in the world that can raise that baby the way you were meant to. You're already a perfect match for one another, because that little soul was placed with you instead of someone else. Do you know how many millions of mothers it could have been sent to? But it was sent to you. So just love it, and do your very best every single day, and everything will be just as it should be."

She leaned against my shoulder, soaking my sleeve with tears. "Oh my God, Grace. That was sooo," she paused to sniffle and sob, "good." More sniffles. "Really. You should put that on a card or something. Thank you."

I patted her back gently and, looking at the camp that was slowly being assembled off the back of the castle, decided it best to change the conversation to help pull her out of her sulk. "So tell me a little bit about who will be here. It's all pretty hard to keep up with."

She laughed and nodded, wiping her eyes as she lifted herself off me. "Yes, it is. You don't need anything to explain your family's appearance here, or mine. Everyone will think we talk funny, but I've found if you just say that you grew up far away from here, people don't seem to question it too much. It's really with the Conalls and MacChristys that things get complicated—seeing as Bri and Blaire are uncanny look—alikes."

They truly were. "How so?"

"Well, Blaire is Donal MacChristy's real daughter and, until Bri's appearance, everyone thought he had just one. But they look so much alike that they couldn't very well say they weren't twins. No one would believe it."

It seemed a very tricky situation. "So how does one go about making everyone who's known the family their whole life believe that Donal had a secret daughter?"

"Good question. You don't. I mean, they've created a story, but anyone with half a brain questions it. Luckily, no one is apt to question Laird Conall, Laird MacChristy, or his brother, Lennox."

"There are two MacChristys?" Sheesh, I needed a notebook.

"Donal has a brother, you see. Here's how they now explain Bri: Donal's wife died giving birth to Blaire, but now he says that she gave birth to twins, and he was so worried about raising two daughters on his own that he sent one of them away to live with his brother, Lennox MacChristy."

"Of course."

She laughed, appreciating my sarcasm. "Yes. Naturally. Anyway, Lennox MacChristy is a perpetual nomad. He's moved his three sons all over the globe their entire lives, so it's not as if many people could prove that he'd not raised Donal's secret daughter."

"Ah." Slowly, it made more sense.

"Yes. Anyway, that's who is coming to the gathering. Donal's brother hasn't been in this part of Scotland in a long time. Since Donal and all of the Conalls are already here, it seemed the perfect time for one big ass family reunion."

"Okay. Anybody else I should know about?"

"The Camerons will be coming as well."

"The Camerons?"

Mitsy nodded, pointing into the woods. "Yes. Pretty small group, but still, they'll be here. Kenna's sister Nairne," a shadow of the still new wound crossed Mitsy's face but she masked it well, "she's dead now and so is her son, both by Niall's hand. Her widowed daughter-in-law, Wynda, still resides at Cameron Castle. She will be here with her children."

I couldn't imagine such loss or such evil. Niall had torn so many lives apart, lives that were still struggling to heal.

Mitsy must have been able to read my thoughts, for she echoed just exactly what I'd been thinking. "He was an evil bastard. I hope he rots in hell."

"I don't blame you." Eoghanan's scar flashed before my eyes, a permanent reminder of all the destruction Niall had caused. "I'm glad he's dead, too."

Chapter 32

"Look at him." Eoghanan's arms came around me and I leaned into him, taking his hands in mine as I pointed in Jeffrey's direction.

The gathering was now in full swing. The castle had been turned into a constant bustle of activity. The grand dining hall was filled with people visiting, laughing, dancing, and, in Jeffrey's case, flirting rather obviously.

"Aye, I see him. What about it?"

I couldn't pull my eyes away from them. The way he fawned over the widow Wynda Cameron, smiling and lingering, it was like watching a zoo animal. "I've never seen him like that. He really likes her."

"Wynda?" Eoghanan's voice echoed surprise.

I jerked my head to the side as he spoke loudly into my ear.

"Yes. Wynda. Someone just offered him food, and he dismissed it. I think he's quite taken with your cousin, Eoghanan."

He nipped playfully at my ear, while he thumbed the bottom of my breast that lay hidden beneath his arm. "Aye, well I doona think she's taken a liking to him yet. She looks verra…distressed."

I nodded, my sympathy for Jeffrey building. For all his proclamations that he was an expert in such areas, he was as out of practice as I was. "Yes, I can see that, too. Should we maybe save him from embarrassment?"

"No, I doona think so. I've need of ye at the moment." He pressed his hips subtly against my backside, and the hard rod lodged between us showed me what he meant.

"Are you crazy? Not here."

He laughed. "No, o'course no right here. I am no an

animal, Grace. Come with me."

"Wait. Where's Cooper? Jeffrey's clearly distracted." I had a hard time pulling my eyes away from the train wreck.

"Last I saw him, he was torturing Lady Blaire. He'll keep himself occupied, Grace. I havena seen ye in days. I only wish to steal ye away for a few moments."

I faced him and wrapped my arms around him. "You've seen me every day. I've been sleeping right next to you."

"Aye, but we've truly been sleeping, 'tis the problem. Readying for visitors has exhausted us all far too much. I am no so tired this night."

I was ready to spend some time alone with him as well. Though I'd gone years without male companionship, it was as if once awakened to it, I couldn't go long without him before I started to feel a bit empty. I reached around and playfully cupped his rear end. "Neither am I. Let's go."

He groaned as he pulled me away, but we only got a few steps before we walked right into Lennox MacChristy and his three sons.

"Eoghanan, what a fine man ye've turned into. Do ye remember me, son?"

Eoghanan pulled upright and moved so that I stood in front of him, hiding his lower half.

"Aye, o'course I do. It has been a long time."

The old man laughed and his round stomach continued to shake after he stopped laughing. "Aye, I think ye were no older than seven the last time I passed through these parts, and me sons werena with me then. Let me introduce ye."

"I'm sorry." Eoghanan held up a hand to stop him.

I glanced up at him confused. It was very unlike him to be so abruptly rude.

"I'm afraid 'twill have to wait. There is something I must attend to right away."

He nodded at the group of men and quickly pulled me away, dragging me across the room toward a small alcove draped in darkness.

"Eoghanan, what's the matter with you? I think you could've waited the five minutes it would have taken to introduce yourself."

He nodded in the direction we were headed. "No, 'tis Cooper."

It was then that I noticed him standing with his back pressed against the side of the archway, looking up at the tall young woman standing in front of him. At first glance, there was nothing menacing about the situation. He chatted with the woman just as comfortably as he did everyone else. It was Eoghanan's urgency that unnerved me.

"Do you know her?"

"No. I havena met her. I know all who should be here, and she is no among them."

He approached them, and I didn't miss the look of alarm in the woman's eyes as he did so. Eoghanan might not have known her, but she knew him well enough.

"Is this yer son? We were just discussing our shared love of partridge."

I looked at Cooper who locked eyes with me and subtly shook his head. I immediately stepped forward to grab his hand, answering before Eoghanan got the chance. "No, he's my son. I'm Grace." I extended my hand. "You are?"

"Just a traveler. Me name is no important."

"Aye, lass. I'm afraid 'tis. Do ye no live in the village?" Eoghanan took one step in her direction, placing himself between me and Cooper.

"Mom, I don't even know what partridge is. Is that like a bird, because I never said I liked a partridge?" He whispered it quietly to me.

I squeezed his hand and nodded. "I know."

Taking in our exchange, the woman realized she'd been caught in a lie and slowly backed away. "No, I doona live in the village. I am only passing by and noticed the gathering."

167

Eoghanan held his arm out and moved with her toward the outside doors. "Then, I think it best ye be on yer way. Safe travels."

Cooper and I stood waiting as Eoghanan showed the woman outside. I bent to pick Cooper up, trying to get a read for how he felt.

"What did she say to you, Coop?"

"Umm…" he lifted his shoulders in a shrug. Clearly the encounter had freaked me out much more than it had him. "She just asked me if E-o was my dad or something. When I said no, she asked me who was and then you guys walked up."

He squirmed in my grasp. No matter how much I didn't want to admit it, he wasn't going to allow me to keep picking him up very much longer.

"Can you put me down, Mom? I don't want people to see you carrying me around. Besides, I gotta go find Dad."

"Why? What are you and Dad doing?"

"He said for the next dance he'd carry me on his shoulders."

I lowered him to the ground, and he danced off in his father's direction as Eoghanan walked back toward me.

"What the hell was that?"

"I doona know for sure, but I believe 'twas the witch Niall went to for his poisons; a witch who is verra soon to be dead."

Chapter 33

"I'm sorry. Say that again. The witch who gave Niall the poisons that killed Osla, incapacitated you, and made your mother ill is still alive?" It seemed unlikely that even with Eoghanan gone, that Baodan wouldn't have gone after the woman with a vengeance.

"Aye, Baodan had her cottage raided soon after they sent me forward but she was gone, and no one has seen her since. I hoped Niall had killed her before the end. He would have, had he succeeded."

I ran my hands up and down my arms to rub away the cold that had crept over my limbs. "Why would she come back here?" It didn't make sense to me. It seemed like an accomplice to murder would flee and never come back.

"I doona know. It worries me. I have no laid eyes on the lass until tonight, and I dinna like to see her with Cooper."

"No." I shook my head as Eoghanan, pulled me in close to him. "I didn't either. Cooper said she wanted to know if you were his father. Why would she ask that?"

His chin rested on the top of my head, and he twisted in gently. "I doona know. When the gathering is over, we will find her again. We canna do it now, for there are many here from the villages who have used her services before. She may have unlikely friends."

* * *

The search of the grounds took longer than he'd hoped, but it was worth it to ensure that everyone was safe. Eoghanan expected Cooper and Jeffrey were already abed, but he couldn't bring himself to wait another night to speak with them both.

He heard Cooper's voice on the first knock and breathed a little easier knowing he wouldn't be responsible for waking the child, especially when the little lad slept so little to begin with.

"You want me to get it, Dad?"

Jeffrey's voice neared the doorway. "No, Coop. I got it. You just stay where you're at."

Eoghanan stepped back as the door opened. "I'm sorry to disrupt ye. Might I speak a moment with ye both?"

Jeffrey motioned for him to enter and Eoghanan moved inside where he was immediately forced to open his arms to catch the young child flying toward him as he jumped off the bed.

"Cooper, do ye no think 'tis past yer bed time?"

"Well usually, but tonight was a special night."

"Aye, 'twas indeed. I'm glad that I've found ye awake. I need to speak with ye and yer da."

Eoghanan turned to Jeffrey's voice. "Is something wrong? Is Grace okay?"

It was Cooper's voice that answered Jeffrey. "Everything's fine, Dad. Look at his face. If something was wrong, he'd look worried. He just looks kinda nervous."

Jeffrey moved to stand in front of him and Cooper, reaching out to mess with his son's hair. "You are too perceptive, kiddo." Jeffrey looked away from his son, turning his attention to Eoghanan. "Why are you nervous?"

"'Cause he likes Mom." Cooper shook his head dramatically, speaking before Eoghanan had the chance. "And I mean *really* likes her. Isn't that right E-o?"

Eoghanan moved to stand Cooper back on the bed, preferring to speak with them while he faced them both. "Aye, 'tis yer mother I wish to speak to ye both about."

"Okay. Let's hear it." Jeffrey crossed his arms waiting for Eoghanan's explanation. Cooper glanced over at his father and mimicked him, crossing his own arms right alongside him.

Taking a breath for courage, Eoghanan spoke. "I know

that the three of ye are a family, and I want ye to know that I doona ever wish to disrupt it, but 'tis me hope that ye are open to adding another member. I am verra much in love with Grace. I canna imagine me life without her," he glanced at Cooper, "or ye Cooper. 'Tis me intention to ask her to marry me, but I willna do so without having both yer blessing."

Cooper smiled back at him. "Whoa. That's a big question, E-o."

Jeffrey continued to regard him pensively, his arms crossed, guarded. "So are you saying that if either of us said no, you really wouldn't ask her? That's a big statement, my man."

Eoghanan nodded. He wouldn't. Committing to Grace meant committing to her family, and he wanted both of them to accept him willingly. "Aye, I wouldna. I give ye me word."

"But Dad..." Cooper reached out to tug on his Dad's arm. "You already told me we were gonna stay, so we're gonna tell him yes, right?"

Eoghanan did his best not to smile, wishing to allow Jeffrey the chance to answer.

Jeffrey turned to speak below his breath to Cooper but did it so that Eoghanan could hear him. "Well, of course we're going to tell him yes, but I was just trying to make him sweat a little."

"That's not very nice, Dad." Cooper lifted one eyebrow, a gesture of disapproval, in his father's direction.

"You're right. It's not." Jeffrey turned back toward Eoghanan. "Yes, you have our full permission to ask her to marry you. I think you're a good man, Eoghanan. Do not prove me wrong."

Eoghanan extended a hand in his new friend's direction. "I swear to ye that I will do everything in me power to make her happy."

Jeffrey took his hand, shaking it just a little too firmly. "I'm serious, okay? I don't care if you're six inches taller than me and the size of a professional football player. You hurt Grace, and I will hurt you. Understood?"

"Aye, I do. It pleases me that Grace has so many that care for her." Eoghanan stepped toward Cooper, shaking his little hand as well to seal their agreement. "I will bid ye goodnight now. I thank ye both."

Eoghanan shut the door behind him, but not before he heard Cooper's little voice laughing at his father.

"You're a funny guy, Dad. You wouldn't even step on that spider earlier. I mean, come on, what do you think you're gonna do to E-o?"

Chapter 34

It took me the rest of the evening to wrangle my stress over the incident to a manageable size. I couldn't stand the thought of someone so evil standing so close to my son. Eoghanan had left immediately to find Baodan, and together they went with a small group of men to ensure she hadn't remained anywhere on the property.

When I saw Jeffrey leave the dining hall with Cooper in tow, I decided to take my leave as well, stopping to ensure they made it safely to their bedchamber before making my way up to Eoghanan's room.

Once inside, I didn't bother to disrobe before collapsing onto the center of the large bed, the stress of the evening making me weak-limbed and exhausted. I wouldn't sleep, not until the men were back and I knew that the grounds were safe. Still, I tried to unwind a bit by rubbing my eyelids with my thumb and middle finger, allowing my fingers to gently rub against my closed eyes.

The repetitive motion must have done the trick, for I didn't hear Eoghanan enter until he spoke.

"Are ye trying to poke yer eye out, lass?"

The sound of his unexpected voice made me jump, and I sat up as he neared me, blinking oddly.

"No, but I think I just about managed it just now. You scared me."

"I'm sorry. I meant to be quiet so that if ye were sleeping, I wouldna wake ye."

I stood and moved to him, reaching up to kiss him warmly. "Did you find anything?"

He shook his head, pulling me closer.

"No, I doona think she will be back. Ye needn't worry yerself over it."

I didn't think for a moment that he really believed what he said. He was too smart not to realize that she wouldn't have taken such a risk to come here unless it was for a reason. Still, there was nothing to be done about it tonight, and I didn't wish to think about it anymore. "Distract me." My voice came shaky, breathless, and desperate. I needed the comforting refuge of his body.

His breath caught, and he lifted my chin from its resting place against his chest. "Distract ye?" He smiled mischievously. "I am sorry, but I canna do it tonight. I'm far too sleepy."

"Oh," I stepped away from him, my eyes teasing, "that's just really too bad. I thought we could play a game, but if you're too sleepy…" I turned away, smiling to the wall as I waited for him to respond.

It took about half a second before he grabbed my wrist and spun me to him. "A game, lass? What sort of game?"

"Well, there's still so many things we don't know about one another. Let's play a game of questions."

He nodded. "Aye, fine, but that doesna sound like a game, Grace. 'Tis a conversation."

"You're right," I pointed at him, excitedly, "but it becomes a game if we go put on every piece of clothing we can stuff ourselves in and then if I want to ask you a question, I have to take off a piece of clothing and you have to do the same."

His eyebrows rose humorously high. "Is this a game often played in yer own time, lass?"

"No, not really. Wanna play?"

"Do ye promise me that we will both end with no any clothes on?"

I nodded, slowly.

"Aye, then I'd verra much like to play yer little game."

* * *

Ten minutes later, we faced each other and instantaneously burst into laughter. We looked equally ridiculous.

I'd squeezed myself into three of Mitsy's dresses which I wore on top of the outfit I'd travelled here in—a bra and underwear, jeans and a t-shirt, with socks, tennis shoes. I also pinned up my hair with every bobby pin that I'd had in my hair on the night of our journey here.

Eoghanan had far less—a pair of linen pants paired with a linen shirt, and two kilts draped oddly around him.

"Tell me the rules of this game, lass, so that we may both play fairly."

"Only this—we each must answer every question completely truthfully." I began to sweat profusely. Perhaps I'd not thought it through perfectly.

"Can we ask one another anything?"

"Yes, anything, but it looks like I'm going to get to ask a lot more questions than you are." I fanned myself, the back of my neck growing sticky.

"I doona need many questions, lass. I already know what I wish to ask ye."

"Is that so? Ok, shoot."

"Shoot?" His brows pulled together in confusion.

"It just means 'start'."

"Oh, aye, fine. Me first question is this," he paused and removed the first kilt. "Do ye miss yer own time, Grace?"

"No." My answer slipped out even more easily than I'd expected, but it was true. "There are exactly three things I miss about the twenty-first century." I hesitated. "Okay, maybe more than three, but only three that seem very significant to me. Number one, refrigerator ice; number two, toothpaste; number three, Bebop."

I started pulling the first dress off my shoulders, but Eoghanan held out a hand to stop me. "No so fast. I still have three questions left."

I'd assumed we would alternate questions, but he seemed so eager to continue that I stopped messing with the laces and went back to fanning myself.

After a moment of maneuvering, the second kilt dropped. "I couldna love Cooper any more if he was me own, but this is me second question—do ye wish for more children, Grace?"

I grew even warmer, my heart beating quickly at the happiness that filled it at Eoghanan's confession. I loved how he loved Cooper. "Yes, bukoos more."

He smiled, and I knew that my answer pleased him. I could see the future children I'd always dreamed of, all with the same red hair, same full lips as Eoghanan. I wanted those children to be his.

Slowly, he removed his linen shirt. "Me third question is this—do ye trust me to care for ye and Cooper? To love ye and protect ye and be there for ye always?"

It was more than one question, but I said nothing about it, my head getting a bit light as he walked toward me, gathering up my hands as he stared at me with pleading eyes.

"Yes, Eoghanan, I trust you completely."

"And I, ye, lass. I have one question left, but I doona wish to ask it in the nude. Me fourth question is this—will ye marry me?"

Chapter 35

It certainly wasn't the way I'd ever imagined a proposal—with me feeling like an overweight *Barbie*, the layers of clothes making me look puffy and foolish, while the man I loved stood before me half naked, looking as handsome as I'd ever seen him. Still, it was sweet and perfect, and whether it was sweat or tears I couldn't be sure, but my eyes were wet as I answered him.

"Yes." I stepped forward to kiss him, my hands struggling to reach his face amongst the heavy weight of the sleeves. "I would love nothing more, but I think there's someone else you might need to speak to before we make it completely official."

He brushed a tear away from my cheek and nodded while he smiled down at me. "Aye, two others that I counted. I've already spoken to both Cooper and Jeffrey."

"No you haven't?" I kissed him again. He was always thoughtful; it shouldn't continually surprise me, but every time it did.

"Aye, and they have both given their blessing. Though, if I hurt ye, Jeffrey has promised to cause me great harm."

I laughed but had to step away to fan myself again. "I'm sure he had you shaking in your boots, huh?"

His eyebrows pinched together in the adorable way they always did when he didn't understand one of my modern expressions.

"Never mind. I love you."

"And I love ye, lass. Ye will never truly know just how much."

I pinched the fabric in between my bosom and lifted it up and down trying to prevent heatstroke. "I don't mean to spoil the moment, but I think it's my turn in this game. If not, I'm going to pass out."

He looked at me playfully and slowly removed his pants, completing his last question. He walked slowly to the bed. It was utterly astonishing at how little his rear end jiggled as he did so. The man was an unbelievable specimen.

He stretched casually and confidently over the bed, lying on his side and propping his head up on his hand while watching me closely. "Please lass, 'tis now yer turn. Ask me whatever ye wish."

Compared to his questions, mine seemed like fluff, but to me they weren't. I could tell a lot about a person by the small stuff.

Gleefully, I shed the first dress, instantly feeling ten pounds lighter. "Okay," I said, shaking myself out, allowing a breeze to work its way under the fabric. "First question. Do you like dogs?"

I'd never had one myself, although I'd always wanted one. I didn't trust anyone that said no to that question.

"Aye, there are few animals that I doona like."

"Good answer." I kicked off my tennis shoes, sending them sailing across the room. "Second question. When you're holding a child and they decide to use your sleeve…" I paused thinking on his normal attire, "okay, let's pretend that you're usually wearing a shirt. Anyhow, a child decides to use your sleeve as a nose tissue, are you quick to anger and disgust?"

He laughed loudly, emphasizing the tight muscles in his stomach. "Why would I get angry, lass, when I use me shirt for just the same purpose?"

I let loose one uncomfortable chuckle, praying that he joked. I didn't ponder the thought long, slipping happily out of the second dress. "Question number three. What was your father like?"

In my opinion, this was perhaps the most important question. Men often turned into their dads, just like women did their mothers. If my parents had birthed boys, I had no doubt they would have turned into mini-me, terrifying versions of my father, just as Jeffrey had become the most admirable of men like his own.

"Ah. I doona believe we have spoken of this before. The father that raised me was a kind, honest, decent man, but he was no me father by birth."

"Oh." Another reason, perhaps, that Eoghanan had taken so graciously to my strange relationship with Jeffrey. He too had grown up with another man standing in the stead of his real father. "So, did you know your real father?"

He clucked his tongue at me and pointed to my still overly-dressed body. "That was another question, was it no? I think ye must remove something else before I answer."

I grasped at the opportunity and shed the last remaining dress, standing before him in my jeans and t-shirt. "Gladly. Now answer."

"No, I doona know who me real father was. Me mother worked for the McMillans and when she became pregnant, they protected her. After she died giving birth to me, they took me in and raised me as their son."

I pointed to his red, curly mane, which was already starting to grow rather unruly, despite the recent cut it had received. "I should have realized, with the red hair and all. You look nothing like Baodan." He nodded but said nothing so I removed my socks in preparation for the next question. "Okay, would you rather be hot or cold?"

"Cold."

Fair enough. I removed my shirt. "Next question. What's your biggest pet peeve?"

His brows pinched in again. "I doona know what a 'peeve' is, lass."

"What's the one thing that drives you crazy? That you can't stand?"

"Ah. The sound of rain."

My hands flew up in surprise and my voice came out all high and pitchy. "What? Who doesn't like the sound of rain?"

179

"Me, lass. The sound of rain makes me think of water, and I doona like to swim. That and it always makes me need to relieve meself something dreadful."

"That is so weird. Sorry, but that's one strike."

"What do ye mean, by strike?"

I was really going to have to cool it with the modern references. "It's a sports thing. If you get three strikes, you're out."

He lifted off of his hand suddenly and swung himself so that he sat up on the edge of the bed. "Out, lass? Are ye giving me some sort of test? Ye do know that ye've already agreed to marry me, aye?"

"Yeah, but two more strikes, and I'm gonna have to back out."

"'Tis no an option, Grace. Just remove your bottoms and ask yer next question."

I winked at him. "Okay, I think this is my last question, actually. Then maybe you can just remove everything else. That sound okay?"

His eyes were locked on my bra and the cleavage it produced between my breasts. I assumed he didn't mind me handing over the task to him.

"Okay, what do you think the word 'girlfriend' means?"

"'Tis a strange question, lass. Doona ye think the name itself tells its meaning. It refers to lassies who are me friends."

My finger went up like a corrective school teacher. "Wrong. I know that's not a word used here, so it's okay, but let's just clear that up right now. Your girlfriend is what I was to you right before I became your fiancé. The first time you used that word in front of me, I thought you were gleefully admitting to sleeping with your brother's wife."

His lusty, half-closed eyes, suddenly opened to the size of saucers. "Ach, I dinna ever mean that."

"Yeah, I know. Now come here."

He stood and moved over to me, reaching around to the

clasp of my bra as he reached me. I leaned up to kiss his neck, trailing kisses up to his ear so that I could whisper into it.

"I have one last question. Bottom or top?"

Chapter 36

Sleepless nights filled with love making differed greatly from sleepless nights in the office working on magazine articles or sleepless nights tending to a sick child. When the sun rose the next morning and my eyes had yet to close for a single minute, I realized that while my body was beyond exhausted, my mind was alert and happy.

"What's the plan for the day?" I rolled to face him, Eoghanan's deep green eyes piercing into my soul.

He said nothing for a moment, and I could sense that he hesitated. "No verra much. If ye doona mind, I'd like to make the announcement of our coming marriage today."

I didn't mind at all. If Vegas was only an airplane away rather than several hundreds of years, I would have suggested we marry the very next day. I moved to run my hands through his hair, kissing his nose as I snuggled into him. "I don't mind at all. How soon can we be married? I mean, I'm not very familiar with how weddings work here."

He rolled over onto his stomach, propping himself up on his elbows as he looked down at me. "As soon as ye wish, lass. I dinna wish to rush if ye wanted to take some time, but I'd marry ye today if I could."

"Today? Could things be arranged so quickly?" I closed my eyes and smiled, delighting in the feeling of his fingertips as he ran feather light touches up and down my bare arm.

"'Tis no so much to arrange, but I'm afraid I must leave for a day or two to make special preparations."

"Preparations for what?" Fear that I'd managed to lock away for the night crept back. "You're not…Eoghanan, I don't want you to go after her."

"No, lass. I am no afraid of the witch, Jinty. Without me brother to act as her puppet master, I doona think she is capable of real harm. Though should I get the chance to end her life, I will do so for all the pain she helped bring upon this family. 'Tis only that I wish to prepare a surprise for ye. Baodan and I will leave this afternoon."

I knew it was ridiculous. I was too grown to allow such a notion to find a resting place in my mind, but the thought of him being away for a mere two days made me rather sad. "Must you leave? In the middle of the gathering?"

"Doona worry yerself, Grace. The gathering will last for weeks. Few will even notice our departure. Eoin and Arran will be here to care for things in our absence. Trust me, when ye see what I've planned for ye, ye will be glad I left." He flipped over onto his back and stood rather abruptly. "In the meantime, I need ye to stay here a moment while I check on yer other surprise."

He dressed quickly and left, leaving me with a mind full of confused wonderings. He'd not left my side all night. How could he have so many plans already in place?

He didn't leave me long to imagine what he had planned, arriving back in the doorway within a matter of minutes, the largest smile I'd ever seen on his face.

"I think ye best get dressed, Grace."

I stood and did as he asked. His excitement roused my curiosity greatly. "Okay, what is it? What have you done?"

He shrugged nonchalantly. "'Tis no so much what I have done, but Morna. Ye see, I had a conversation with wee Cooper before we traveled back here, and he spoke of a man verra important to ye all. When I told Morna of him, she promised that she would check in often to see how things progressed between us and should they lead to marriage, she would send ye, Cooper, and Jeffrey a gift. Yer gift has arrived."

Surely he couldn't mean what he made it sound like. The man who the three of us leaned on more than any other and the last missing piece in our little puzzle couldn't possibly be here.

I fumbled with the laces in my anticipation and eventually spun my back toward Eoghanan, lifting my hair and pointing to my back. "Help me, please."

He obliged, working quickly with the laces. "There. Ye are properly covered and free to go and see yer surprise. I hope ye are no disappointed."

I hoped so, too. He'd built up to it so much, making me believe it could only be one thing, that I knew if it wasn't I would have a difficult time masking my disappointment.

I walked quickly down the hallway, unsure of just where my surprise lay. Then I heard it—the same voice that I'd gone to my entire life for guidance and comfort, the same voice that Cooper loved second only to mine and Jeffrey's.

I turned the corner and nearly wept. There, with Cooper clinging to him, grasping his neck so tightly I was surprised he could breathe, stood Bebop.

* * *

"So one day, I was sitting on my back deck fishing, and I closed my eyes for just a moment," Bebop winked at me, "resting my eyes as I do, and the next moment I'm sitting in a stranger's living room with an old man and woman staring back at me."

He had us all enraptured, Cooper, Jeffrey, Eoghanan and me all standing around him, listening intently to his tale of how Morna had brought him here. He had the unique ability to tell any story, even everyday stories that weren't truly as interesting as the one he told now, as if they were the grandest of tales.

No wonder my son had such a vivid imagination and that he'd developed an early love of books. Who wouldn't with a grandfather like that to tell you stories? He was the sort of man one could listen to for hours.

Bebop, whose real name was Charles Oakes, was a good decade older than both of my parents. He and Maggie had given birth to Jeffrey later in life, after over a decade of trying to have children. Bebop stood the same average height as Jeffrey, about five-seven, although his shoulders now hunched a little, making him look shorter than he really was. An avid cyclist, he was in phenomenal shape for a man his age, but he still looked very grandfatherly—like a surprisingly sprite Gepetto.

He still had a full head of hair but it was entirely gray, and he wore a pair of spectacles that often lingered on the end of his nose. He continued relaying his tale, laughing as he spoke.

"Well, I'll tell you. For a moment I thought my mind had either caught up with the age of my body, or I'd had a heart attack sitting right on my deck and heaven was just very different than I'd ever imagined it."

Cooper leaned back, still in Bebop's arms and gripped either side of the man's face, as if he couldn't believe he was really here. "So how did she make you believe everything? These two," he pointed to me and his father, "had a real hard time with it."

Bebop leaned in and pressed his forehead to Cooper's, speaking only to him. "Did your mother read you the story that your Dad and I picked out for you?"

Cooper nodded, their foreheads still touching. "Yeah, I loved it, Bebop. When I first saw E-o, I thought maybe he was like that little prince in the book, and he'd come here on a spaceship."

Bebop pulled back, his cheeks still framed by Cooper's little hands. "Well, I'm not ruined like the grown-ups in the book. I can still see things like a child. I've always believed in a bit of magic." He turned his head to the side to look at us 'ruined,' grown-ups. "But, I'll tell you. I don't know if I could have dreamed up something like this. How very exciting. Now," he shifted Cooper into his left arm and reached up to grip his head with his right hand. "I need someone around here

185

to give me something to help with this bloody bad headache."

Chapter 37

"How's my sweet girl doing? You look stunning."

I turned and threw my arms around Bebop, still stunned and delighted at his sudden appearance here. "I'm great. How's your head?"

"Oh, that," he dismissed it with his hand, "much better actually. I have to tell you Grace, the last time I saw you in a dress about to walk down the aisle, the sight made me ill."

I snorted, laughing into his shoulder. It had made me ill as well. "Geeze, thanks."

"You know what I mean, Grace. My heart was broken for you that you planned to do something so foolish as to marry my son. This is very different. I don't pretend to know the man you plan to marry, but it feels very right to me. And my gut is always right."

It was. Bebop's advice was something I'd never taken lightly.

"Thank you. I can't tell you how glad I am that you're here. It seems rather impossible to me."

"Less impossible to you than me, I imagine. Childlike I may be, but truthfully, all of this is a lot to take in." He paused, releasing me so that I could take one last glance in the mirror. "Can I tell you a story?"

I would never turn down a Bebop story. "Of course you can."

"Good. Are you ready? I'll tell you while we walk down if you are."

"Yes." I smiled and looped my arm in his.

I wasn't altogether sure where exactly the wedding would take place. We'd announced our impending nuptials the morning after Bebop arrived, but had decided to have a private ceremony with only the closest of family. Cooper, Jeffrey, and

Bebop on my side. Baodan, Mitsy, and Kenna on Eoghanan's.

As a result, there'd been very little to prepare, and I gladly allowed Eoghanan to plan all of the little surprises he seemed so intent upon.

As we moved down the hallway from the bedchamber where I'd readied myself with the help of Mitsy and Kenna, Bebop began his story. "Do you remember what I told you when you were pregnant with Cooper? When you were so worried that you would be a terrible mother?"

I smiled, he had no way of knowing just how well I remembered every word of what he'd told me that day. "Of course I do."

"Maggie hated that story. It was what I used to tell myself every time she miscarried. For all those years that we tried to have a child, I would rationalize the loss by saying, 'that soul wasn't meant for us. Ours is coming.' I could always tell it made her angry. She felt that me saying that made it seem like children born to abusive, cruel parents were meant to be placed in such situations, and she couldn't stand it. Of course, that's not how I meant it. It's just something that made me feel like I hadn't lost something; that the person meant for me was still on its way to us. And of course he was—Jeffrey."

By this point we were already nearing the main doorways of the castle, and it surprised me to find the hallways and other rooms entirely empty. Either there would be many more guests at our wedding than I anticipated, or they'd been instructed to clear out until after the wedding. I hoped it was the latter. Still, I could tell we neared our destination, for Bebop slowed his pace markedly, clearly not finished with his story.

"As I said, Maggie hated when I would say that, taking my words too literally when they were only meant to soothe my heart each time after a new loss. She never said anything about it though until after you had entered our life."

I couldn't imagine what I had to do with it.

"We already had Jeffrey at that point, but to our surprise

Maggie became pregnant again, only to miscarry the child a few weeks later. As per usual, I said something about the child not being meant for us and for the first time in a decade, she lost it on me. She said that I was a fool to think such a thing when we had the likes of you to show us what an untrue notion that was.

"She said that anyone with half a brain could see that your parents didn't come close to deserving you and that if you were meant to be anyone's child, it was ours." He paused and brought my hand up to his lips, kissing it gently. "I understood then how stupid it was, but it had brought me comfort when I needed it so I never spoke it again until I told it to you when you were pregnant because really, Maggie, was right."

I'd never looked at it as Maggie had either, but it was certainly a way of thinking that could be seen from several viewpoints. As a soon-to-be mother I'd taken it as Mitsy had, words to calm my doubt that I could be the mother I wanted to be for my child. For someone more empathetic to the woes of others, as Maggie had been, or as a child who'd grown up under terrible circumstances, I could see how the thought could be seen as placing uncalled for guilt on a blameless child. No child is meant to grow up in anything less than a loving and caring home.

Still, I didn't understand what him telling me all of this had to do with my getting married in a matter of moments. "Okay, forgive me, Charles. What are you trying to say?"

"Only this, Grace." He stopped walking.

I looked up to see where we were. We were just at the end of the path leading to the secluded tree with the low sitting branch—Eoghanan's special place of thinking where he'd taken me the night Cooper and Jeffrey had disappeared. It would be good to make a new, happier, less-stressed memory in that place.

"That is always how Maggie saw you…as hers, no matter who you were born to. While I know that your real parents

189

aren't here to see you marry the man you're meant to, I am here and," he choked up slightly and I squeezed his hands in comfort, "she is watching all of this from heaven and beaming. I couldn't love you or be any more proud of you than I am right now."

I was full out crying now, and Bebop quickly moved to dab the tears from my face, shaking his head in apology. "Forgive me, I'm a stupid man. I didn't mean to make you cry."

"No, you didn't." I leaned forward and kissed him on the cheek. "Thank you. My whole life I wanted to be your child rather than the child of my parents; to know that you wanted me as much as I did you…nothing could be more pleasing to hear." Inhaling to gain my composure, I turned so that I faced the front of the tree-lined path that served as my aisle. "I love you, Charles. Now, let's get me married, shall we?"

* * *

I wondered just how many brides could recall very much about the actual ceremony part of their wedding, for as it drew to a close and Eoghanan leaned in to kiss me, I realized that I'd been rather lost in a haze of happiness, my emotions so swelled that I couldn't remember anything.

I felt his lips touch mine and guilt swarmed me, until he leaned in and whispered in my ear.

"Ye have made me the happiest man in the world, lass. I am now yers forever, and ye are mine."

It didn't matter that I couldn't remember the ceremony, or just exactly what words had been said. The last words he'd whispered to me were what it was about anyway. They were all that truly mattered.

I just wished I could shake the feeling that everything was going too well.

Chapter 38

Eoghanan McMillan was an utter fool if he thought keeping her off McMillan land would protect them. Jinty had other ways to keep herself abreast of what went on in the castle, other ways to look for the perfect opportunity to take the boy.

She'd been right to think the boy was special to him. The warning in his eyes had been clear enough the day he'd seen her inside the castle. She'd known he suspected who she was. It didn't matter in the least.

She watched them now; Eoghanan and his new bride riding away from the castle. They would be gone for days, the boy left in the care of his real father, a man far less threatening than Eoghanan. She'd continue to watch the child closely and, at the opportune time, she would take him away.

Eoghanan would return to find his new son gone.

* * *

"If ye look back in the direction of the castle once more, lass, I shall turn me horse around and we will go home."

"I'm sorry." I turned my head around and leaned back into him, kissing the underside of his chin. McMillan Castle was far from view by now but, for whatever reason, looking back toward the castle helped to ease my nervousness at leaving Cooper.

He'd be fine, of course. He stayed with his father at least two nights a week back in New York, but for some reason, I was irked by an unexplainable sense of worry. Whether it was the newness of our situation or the vastness of the castle and its endless ways for Cooper to get in trouble, I didn't know, but it wasn't fair of me to give Eoghanan anything less than my full attention.

"How much farther are you taking me?" I reached my arms up behind his head, gently massaging the back of his scalp while I leaned into him, just as I'd done the day I'd cut his hair.

He let loose a deep contented sigh of enjoyment. "Ach, Grace, as much as I love the way that feels, I doona think I can stay sitting up properly on me horse if ye continue that."

Following our wedding, we joined the others residing at the castle for the gathering at a large celebratory dinner that lasted well into the wee hours of the morning. We'd collapsed so exhaustedly into bed that thoughts of binding our marriage vows through consummation hadn't crossed our minds for a moment. Now, however, it was all I could think about.

"So why don't you get off your horse for a bit. Seems to me like we've still got quite a ways to go."

"Aye, that we do, Grace. At least a full day more which is why I doona understand why ye think I should get off me horse, 'twould only delay us further."

I laughed against him, rather shocked at his daftness. It was the one thing constantly on the mind of any man and the moment it was so clearly on mine, he couldn't take the hint. I shifted my bottom, rocking it into him a bit to emphasize my point. "Who cares if it delays us a little? I want to be..." I hesitated, trying to think of the word I'd heard once. "What is it that you all say? Tupped? I want to be tupped by my husband."

The catch of his breath was instant and so was the slight pull on the horse's reins. "Tupped is no a kind sort of reference, lass. Ye should be careful saying just what it is that ye want. I doona think 'tis that."

I couldn't tell whether he meant it as a challenge or he just didn't wish to get his hopes up, but I reached behind him and pulled at the hair along the base of his neck. "I don't think it's really your place to tell me what I do and don't want. I'm more than capable of figuring that out for myself. And right now…I don't want to be cherished. I don't want to be caressed or taken slowly…"

He pulled the horse to a stop before I even finished. "Right now, I want to be claimed by my husband. I want you to throw me up against one of these trees and take me so roughly that the only way I can sit this horse again is by sitting sideways." He nearly choked on his own spit, and his breathing came ragged in my ear.

"I want my *husband,*" I emphasized the word, drawing it out and speaking in the most seductive voice I could manage. It sounded rather ridiculous to me, but it seemed to do the trick for him just fine. "To fu…"

Finally, he spoke, flinging himself off the side of the horse so that he could pull me off with him. "Ach, hush yer mouth, Grace. I doona even know what to say to ye. I have never in me life heard a lass speak such."

His tone was admonishing, but he still hurriedly pulled me toward a secluded area amongst the trees, his chest rising and falling quickly with each step. He didn't look back at me until he stopped walking, spinning to force my back against a wide-based tree, his cheek leaning forward to press flush against mine. "'Tis verra shocking."

"Is it?" I enjoyed this exchange so different from any we'd had before. The evening he'd been drunk, he'd kissed me roughly—his own inhibitions dampened enough by the ale to permit him to treat me less gently than he had at any time since that night. I'd enjoyed that brief encounter very much. Every woman wanted to be cared for, to have a man take their time with them, and Eoghanan certainly did both of those things. In this instance, however, I didn't want to be taken slowly. Now that Eoghanan was my husband, I wanted him to know that I trusted him to do with me what he wished. I wanted to feel as if I belonged to him and him alone. I wanted to be claimed by him.

"Aye, 'tis Grace. I canna tell if ye speak in jest or no." He leaned his hips into me, the length of him pressing into my abdomen. "Ye see, lass," his voice grew more husky every second, "it doesna matter how good the man, there is a bit of beast in all of us. 'Tis hard enough for us to no treat ye such when we know ye doona wish it; but when ye ask for it, Grace…" he paused, drawing in a shaky breath. "Ye should no tease a man with such things."

I smiled against his cheek, slowly sliding my hand in front of me, bending my knees slightly so that I could reach underneath his kilt and wrap my hand around him. "Do I look like I'm teasing you? I care far too much about you to do that." He groaned into my ear as I rubbed him. "I am entirely serious, Eoghanan. I need you. Now."

He growled and removed my hand from him, raising my dress as he spun me so that my chest and face pressed against the tree.

"As ye wish, lass, but doona say that I dinna warn ye against this."

Chapter 39

"We canna ride the horse the rest of the way. I'll leave him with a man I know in the village. We must make the rest of the way on foot."

I nodded, flipping myself over so that I could slide off the top of the horse. "Thank God." He'd done as I'd asked him, much to my regret, and I had indeed been forced to ride the rest of our journey sideways, my thighs much too sore to spread them over the width of the horse.

After one more day of riding, we arrived at the smallest of villages that sat at the base of a tall cliff. Only one trail led up the hillside. While I could see that was where he intended to take me, I still couldn't make out the final destination.

"Still tender are ye, Grace? I told ye I dinna think 'twas truly what ye wanted. I dinna mean to harm ye, lass." He dismounted and gathered me in his arms, kissing me down the side of my cheek until his lips landed tenderly on my own. "I love ye more than ye can ever know. I would never knowingly hurt ye."

"You didn't. Just bruised me a little. It is not your fault. I brought it on myself." I laughed against him. "I only wish I'd known just what I was asking for. I think perhaps I wanted to behave more adventurously than I truly am."

"Aye, I feel much the same. I willna deny that no matter how I bury meself inside ye, I love it enough to sell me own mother for a chance to do it again, but I want to see yer face when I make love to ye, Grace. I want to touch the verra piece of yer soul that is now shared with me own. 'Tis a wondrous thing that can occur with the pairing of two bodies."

With my face resting against him, I breathed in his heady scent, undeniably male after so many days on the road. He smelled of sweat and earth, and sex. It was a comforting, surprisingly lovely smell, and I loved it. "You know, I don't think there's a single man alive that would admit to feeling that way."

"Aye, and I doona think most men do feel as I do, lass. I am no a common man. 'Tis perhaps the poet in me that makes me so."

"Hicumm...." The deep noise came from behind, and I twisted to find a man in his mid to late forties standing with his arms crossed and a pleased expression in his eyes. "If ye be a poet, then I am Laird of yer brother's castle. Now, introduce me to yer new bride."

Eoghanan stepped away to greet the man but kept one hand on the small of my back, nudging me along with him. "'Tis good to see ye, Tinley. This is me wife, Grace."

I smiled and nodded to him, trying my best not to speak as to rouse the usual conversation that ensued as to the strangeness of my accent.

"Do ye have it ready for us?" Eoghanan moved to bring him the horse as Tinley answered.

"Aye, me wife helped in the preparations. I think ye will find it to yer liking. Doona ye worry about yer beast. I shall take good care of him until ye are ready to return home. There's enough food to last ye a week if ye need it, though I expect the lass will grow tired of ye far earlier than that."

Talk of preparations only heightened my curiosity further. Eoghanan must have sent a rider ahead of us to request such work of Tinley right after we'd announced our wedding for it to be ready and awaiting us today.

Eoghanan handed the reins over and reached for my hand. "I have no doubt that ye are right, but I'll do me best to keep her as long as I can."

"Aye, I'm sure ye shall. She is far too pretty for ye, even before what happened to yer face."

The man's words made me flinch. I'd never known him without the scars, which made it easy to forget that once his face and body had been entirely undamaged by Niall's blade. He looked perfect to me now. The realization that others saw him as injured, as different from how he once was, had trouble resting with me.

No matter what I thought of the man's words, Eoghanan seemed unbothered by them, only nodding in the man's direction as he pulled me toward the winding trail. "Aye, she is. Thank ye for everything. Ye'll find yer payment," he pointed to one of the packs hanging off the horse, "in there."

I waited to speak until Tinley was out of sight, making sure to look down at my feet as I climbed so I wouldn't step on the bottom of my dress. "If you'd warned me, I could have packed my pair of jeans."

He chuckled but continued his trek upward. "No, ye wouldna have. The first time I saw ye in such things I couldna look anywhere but yer thighs and yer backside. I willna have another man see ye dressed in such a way."

I paused for a moment to hike up the dress. "And are there people that would see me dressed in them wherever we are going? I assumed you'd be taking me somewhere a little more secluded."

"Aye, 'tis secluded. I doona wish to see anyone but ye for many days still."

* * *

We marched upward for the good part of an hour before I heard it—the loud rush of water so strong that I couldn't believe I hadn't noticed the sound before. The trail must have wound up the cliffside more than I'd thought, otherwise I couldn't imagine how the sound could have remained so well hidden. "Are we going to a waterfall? Is there a cabin near it that we are staying in or something?"

He slowed for the first time since we'd begun and smiled back at me with a smile that told me I'd still not quite figured it out. "No cabin."

"A castle then? What? A river boat?"

His eyebrows pulled in. "A river boat? No, lass. Why doona ye just wait and see?"

"Patience was never my strong suit."

"Aye, I can see that. But 'tis mine, so no matter how many questions ye ask, I willna say a word. There is no need for ye to ask anything else, for we are there. But first…"

He moved to stand behind me, cupping both hands over my eyes.

"I'll trip if you make me walk like that. My arms are too full of my dress for me to even catch myself."

"I'll catch ye, just step forward and turn when I tell ye to."

He didn't remove his hands from my face until I could feel the spray of the water against my skin. "Now, ye may look."

Chapter 40

Bebop was sleeping, but Cooper could still see that his grandfather was worried. He could tell by the deep lines in his forehead and his wrinkled brow. Cooper knew how he felt. For some reason, he was worried, too.

He approached the chair where Bebop slept quietly, hoping he wouldn't wake him up as he crawled carefully into his lap. He should've known better though. Bebop was always a light sleeper, and his light blue eyes flew open as soon as Cooper settled onto his lap.

"What? Oh good, it's you, Coop. What's my favorite grandson up to? I was just resting my eyes for a while."

Cooper smiled, reaching up to try and stuff the puff of white hair that stuck out the side of his ear back inside. "I'm your *only* grandson, Bebop. And you can't fool me. I know what it means when you say you're resting your eyes—it means that you're sleeping."

Bebop reached up to swat his hand away. "Sleeping? No, I don't sleep during the day."

Cooper didn't argue but nodded to let Bebop know that he knew he did.

"And just because you're my only grandson doesn't mean that you can't be my favorite. What did you and your father do this morning?"

Cooper shifted on Bebop's lap so that he could face him. "We rode with Ba-o into the village and helped him pick up a crib for the baby that's coming. It's really pretty, Bebop. He had some man who can do super cool things with a block of wood make it."

"I should like to see it. Were you a big help?"

Cooper shrugged. He knew he was still too small to be much help to anybody. "I tried but, not really. Hey, can I ask you something, Bebop? What's bothering you so much?"

"What do you mean, son? Nothing's bothering me."

Cooper shook his head. He knew grown-ups sometimes lied to him to protect him, but he didn't like it. "That's not true, Bebop. I've known you my whole life, and I know that you're worried. Now, what's it about?"

Cooper knew the moment Bebop would tell him, because his grandfather reached up to mess with his hair, chuckling slightly as he always did when Cooper surprised him.

"I'll tell you, if I'd been as smart as you are when I was a child, I would have gotten in so much less trouble." Bebop paused. "Or maybe more, hard to tell really. Would you believe me if I told you that you're right when you say I'm worried, but what worries me the most is I don't know why? Just a feeling…like something's coming that I'm powerless to stop. Do you understand that?"

It was like Bebop took the words right out of his head. Cooper nodded and leaned into him. "I do understand. Do you want to know why?"

Bebop reached his arm around him to hug him tight. "Why?"

"Because I feel the same way, Bebop, and I don't know why."

* * *

Brendon Falls

As promised, there was no cabin, castle, or riverboat when I opened my eyes. Instead, I stood perilously close to the edge of the cliff, my feet standing on a small foot-worn trail that seemingly led behind the waterfall. I couldn't see how anybody could make it behind the powerful rush of water without being swept into the water below.

200

"It's beautiful."

His hands slid from my eyes as he moved them down my arms and gathered them around me, pulling me close. "Aye, and so is what lies behind it."

"Behind it?" Even if he and I could manage to follow the trail behind the falls, it would have been impossible for Tinley or anyone else to carry supplies and whatever else they'd left us along that path.

"Aye." He crouched his head down next to mine while I looked nervously at the narrow, rocky trail.

"Well, you go right ahead, mister, because I'm not doing it."

"Do heights frighten ye, Grace?"

"I would be an utter fool if that drop didn't frighten me. Only an idiot would try to walk behind that rushing water." I leaned into him so that he would take a step back. The view was beautiful, but I found myself ready to step away from the ledge.

"Aye, ye are verra right, lass. I wouldna allow ye to get inside the cave by way of the trail even if ye wished it. Do ye no remember when ye fell in me bedchamber at the inn? If ye canna walk across a room without meeting the floor, I doona wish to see ye try to manage that."

I stepped back, pushing us both farther from the ledge. "I remember it very well, but I didn't just fall. I was startled by the sight of you standing there naked."

"Mmmm…"

It was a contented noise, as if the memory brought him great joy. I was sure it did. It was the first day any real flirtation had begun between us. "So, there's a cave behind it, huh? And just how do we get back there?"

He stepped away and took my hand, winking back at me over his shoulder. "This way."

We walked up a rocky staircase that I'd not noticed earlier. At the top, the steps turned downward, leading underneath the river feeding the waterfall. I found the engineering of it amazing, albeit utterly baffling. Without the use of modern tools, it seemed impossible that such a place could exist. "Who did this? It's truly astonishing."

He paused a few steps in front of me, answering over his shoulder. "No one knows. No many know of its existence now. 'Tis truly a place of magic."

I didn't doubt it. As we stepped into the cave itself, I couldn't come up with any other explanation for the dwelling other than the use of magic from another like Morna. "Men didn't create this."

It wasn't a question, and he understood my meaning. "I doona think so, either. 'Twas a question I meant to ask Morna. If she knew of the witch who created this place."

"Perhaps it was Morna." I moved about the room entirely awestruck by its beauty. The magic in the room was tangible.

Candles flickered from every corner of the stone room, highlighting the surprisingly large, round feather bed that sat against the back wall. It was draped in thick coverings, and looking at the warm, lush bed made me realize that I wasn't cold. That in and of itself was enough to convince me of the magic that lingered in the room.

"This is…Eoghanan, I hardly know what to say."

He smiled, leaning a hand against the wall opposite me. "Touch the stones, Grace. 'Tis the only way we could stay so close to the spray and remain warm."

They were warm, almost hot to the touch, and I closed my eyes at the pleasant sensation. "Oh, that's wonderful. I was just wondering at it actually. I wondered how it was that I wasn't freezing in here, so close to the spray of the water."

A warm breath traveled down my neck, and I opened my eyes to find Eoghanan standing over me, his deep green eyes staring into mine. "Are you hungry, lass?"

My stomach seemed to growl on cue, and I laughed into his neck. "Very."

Chapter 41

We were both famished after days on the road and dined happily on an assortment of bread, ale, and meat pies made for us by Tinley's wife – all of it delicious. By the time we'd had our fill, the sun began to dip down into the sky, casting a spectacle of light through the water and into the cave.

I stood from the small table where the food had been so beautifully laid out and ventured nearer the room's edge, hesitantly extending a hand into the running water. Its force sent my hand flying down to my side, but I pulled it upward once again, enjoying the feeling of the water's power running through my fingers, its spray splashing onto my face and body, getting my dress rather wet.

"I think it best ye remove yer dress, before ye soak it so through it willna dry for days."

I laughed but stepped away, reaching behind to work my laces. "True, but if it takes days for my dress to dry, I suppose that also means that I'd be naked for days."

His hands were grasping my arms in an instant. "Too true, lass." He lifted me in the air, swinging me over his shoulder as he stepped into the spray, drenching us both in the cool water.

I gasped and floundered against him, my laughter drowned out by the water that covered us both. Once we were both dripping, he stepped back, setting me on my feet while he laughed deeply enough for the noise to reverberate off the stone.

"What did you do that for? I thought you didn't like water—especially the sound of it falling." I pulled all my hair around over one shoulder, ringing out some of the water.

He removed his kilt unabashedly, his chest still covered with water droplets as he watched me. "I doona like water, but this is a special place and 'tis too beautiful to dislike. Besides,

I would be a damn fool no to stick ye into the waterfall after ye told me that doing so would leave ye naked for days. Do ye know how breathtaking ye are, Grace?"

Despite the cold, heavy dress now glued to my body, I warmed through instantly, blushing as I combed my blonde hair through with my fingers. "Not so breathtaking really, I imagine. You're just partial. You have to say things like that now that I'm your wife."

He crossed his arms while he shook his head, his own red hair dripping and shaggy once more. It grew quickly. Already he neared the need for another cut.

"No, Grace. I doona have to say any such thing to ye. I know plenty of lads who doona think their wives to be pretty and wouldna tell them so just because they were married."

I frowned reactively. "Well, that's quite sad."

"'Tis verra true. I wouldna say it to ye if I dinna mean it, lass. I can scarcely breathe when I stand in front of ye, even dripping like a wet dog as ye are now."

"The wet dog look is your doing. I was content to let the water touch my hands."

"Aye, 'tis. Now, turn around and let me help ye out of yer dress so that we may let it dry."

The laces were difficult to maneuver now that they were wet, but Eoghanan managed them nicely. Once all were untied, he spun me toward him, slowly peeling the heavy fabric off me as if it were a second skin. He paused as he pulled the dress over my breasts, bending down to pull one of my nipples deep into his mouth. The sudden exposure to air tightened them immediately, and the sharp bud flooded with sensation as his lips and tongue moved over it.

My hands moved to his hair, pulling him closer, a silent plea to continue. He rose to kiss me before resuming the work of removing my dress, stepping away once I was fully exposed to him.

"Are ye still too sore, lass?"

"Huh?" The question took a moment to process through my now lusty brain. I was so eager to join him in bed that any lingering soreness had slipped my mind.

"I'm asking ye if ye wish me no to touch ye. I doona wish to hurt ye if ye are still no feeling so well."

One glance down at him told me that regardless of how sore I might be, his current state would have to be attended to.

"No." I walked across the length of the room, passing him as I crawled slowly onto the bed, rolling onto my back once I reached the end. "I'm fine. Just take it more slowly this time."

"Aye," his voice was dry and cracked, his eyes hazy with lust as he moved across the room to join me. "We shall take our time with one another this night, so that we might do that soul reaching that I spoke of."

He ducked his head as he crawled on top of me, taking a moment to search for my soul in between my thighs. He didn't find it, but what he did find made me cry out as I arched beneath him, trembling in response to his touch.

The orgasm helped relax my tightened muscles and readied me for him as he sought his entry. He moved slowly, gently as he promised, never closing his eyes, never changing his rhythm as he waited patiently for me to match him.

I'd thought his words earlier, about what lovemaking could be, lovely. It seemed a nice idea—to think that you could know and love someone so completely that such an act could expose the most sacred part of yourself to that person. But until the sensation built within me, I'd not known if it was truly possible.

It frightened me, the sense of complete connection, simple understanding, and unwavering commitment. As he held onto the side of my face, brushing his thumb over my cheek as he always did to comfort me, I knew that it frightened him, too. What rose within us both paled in comparison to any climax.

In his eyes, I could see what I meant to him – the love,

adoration, and respect he held for me. Unwillingly, it brought tears to my eyes and quickly he kissed them away.

I imagined us to be much like the water in the river above the waterfall, the unexplainable feeling of exhilaration and terror reaching an immeasurable level as we neared the point of falling, of rolling off the cliff's edge.

Our breathing escalated such that it was all I could hear, the sound of the rushing water muted by the noise of our own ragged breath. From somewhere beneath the heart-pounding fog, Eoghanan's voice called out to me, pleading with me to open the eyes I'd not realized I'd closed.

"Doona close yer eyes, Grace. Doona close, them. I need to see ye."

As I opened my eyes, we crashed upon the metaphorical rocks of our lovemaking. We gripped each other as we gasped and trembled, never closing our eyes nor tearing our gaze from the other. Both of us entirely exposed, we found the best parts of ourselves within the soul of the other.

Chapter 42

McMillan Castle

The slip of the poison had been far too easy – into the man's drinking water to settle into his stomach overnight. She'd at least hoped for a challenge, but the end result would be the same. The boy's father would fall ill and lose consciousness for most of the day, allowing her plenty of time to take the lad away before Eoghanan and his new wife returned this evening.

Jinty sat back from her place amongst the trees watching the sunrise in the distance. The boy and his father would do what they did every day after their morning meal—come to sit by the pond. Only this time, they wouldn't be alone. She would be waiting for the poison to go into effect.

* * *

Whatever had worried him and Bebop over the last few days was coming for them today. Cooper didn't know why or what would happen, but he knew it just as sure as he knew he'd love dinosaurs every day of his whole life. There was no other reason why he would have dreamed of the stone.

Everybody thought he couldn't keep secrets, but it was one of the things Cooper was best at. He'd not told Mom that E-o could travel through time or that Morna was a witch when he'd promised them he wouldn't. He'd not told Mom about the time Dad lost him at the city park after he promised Dad he wouldn't. And he'd not told anyone about the story Morna had told him and the promise she'd made him the day he'd thrown the black stone into the pond.

He could remember everything she'd said when she'd

pulled him aside during their tour of the castle.

"Cooper," she'd said to him. "I know that ye took me traveling stones and what ye mean to do with them. Ye are a fine lad, and I trust ye to make the decision ye believe ye must, but I need ye to remember something verra important. Can ye do that for me?"

He loved when grown-ups entrusted him with important tasks. He'd nodded as he answered her. "Of course, I'll remember. I don't forget anything."

"I believe that, lad. Now, this red one here, keep it tucked safely in yer jeans if ye decide to throw the black ones. Yer parents will do all they can to keep ye safe, but sometimes there are things in this world that no one can protect us from. But, ye are luckier than most, lad, for ye have a verra kind and powerful witch watching after ye."

He'd laughed then. He knew that Morna spoke about herself.

"I'll be watching from afar, but I canna keep eyes on ye every moment. Should ye need me, throw this rock into the pond, and I'll come for ye. I have no returned to me own time since I left it, but for ye, child, I'll come running."

That was weeks ago now, but the morning after his dream, right after breakfast he went straight to where he'd last left the rock; his worry still weighing heavily on his little mind. He pulled apart the plastic shell of one of his dinosaur eggs, glancing down at the rock inside. Lifting the shiny, red stone out of its home, he tucked it away just as Dad called to him from the hallway so that they could spend some time at the pond.

Despite all his baby teeth that remained, Cooper had a strong feeling that after today no one would be able to call him a baby. Something bad was coming to the castle and, if he could remember to throw the stone at just the right time, perhaps he could be a hero.

* * *

Our honeymoon continued in a blur of lazy days spent with food, ale, lovemaking, and a surprising lack of sleep. But by the time our clothes had fully dried several days later, we were both ready to return home to Cooper.

I'd never been away from him for so long, and each hoof step that remained until I held him in my arms was one hoof step too many.

"What time do you think we will make it back to the castle?"

Eoghanan had sensed my desire to hurry much earlier, and he'd picked up our pace hours ago.

"This morning I would have told ye nightfall, but we have ridden well throughout the day. I am pleased to tell ye that we approach McMillan territory as we speak, lass."

I looked out over the vast land, the village off to the left, the castle still miles ahead of us. It was a relief to know that I neared my son, and I relaxed a little until smoke billowing up from trees separated from the village caught my attention. There was nothing ominous about the sight, but an inexplicable desire to turn our horse in the direction of the smoke filled me.

"Eoghanan," I pointed in its direction, "what is that over there?"

It took him a moment to respond, and I turned my neck to look up at him.

"I doona know for sure, lass. I know it seems odd, but I have no noticed such a place before. It must be a cottage."

"Could it be?" I didn't want to finish my question, but it was where my mind went immediately. The witch Jinty lived on McMillan territory—Eoghanan had said Baodan had raided her cottage. But surely a witch who knew others were looking for her wouldn't be stupid enough to light a fire that would signal she'd returned home. If the smoke did indeed come from Jinty's cottage, something was very wrong.

"Jinty." Eoghanan's conclusion came just a few seconds

after my own, and his arms grew tense around me as he urged the horse forward more quickly.

He was now as eager to reach the castle as I was.

Chapter 43

Cooper knew his dad could be easily distracted, so when Bebop caught them in the hall on their way out to the pond and started chatting away, Cooper simply smiled, skipping off in the direction of the water alone.

The rock bounced up and down in his pocket, but he kept his hand cupped over it, protecting the magic stone that he knew he would have to use today. He could feel it—the danger coming toward the castle.

Someone meant to harm him; he'd seen the shadow approaching him for nights while he slept. The same scary dream that left him with plenty to think about each morning. He was frightened, but he had to be brave. Bravery was all that would protect him until he sent for Morna, and he knew that even after he threw the rock he would be alone for a time—the travel wasn't always instant.

Cooper rounded the curve that led to the backside of the pond and stopped still. He saw her watching him among the trees, the same lady E-o had forced to leave the castle on one of the nights of the gathering. She couldn't see him looking at her, and he knew that was best. It gave him a moment to think, to gather his courage and slip the rock from his pocket.

Mama never let him watch scary movies, but Dad sometimes did because he knew that Cooper was brave enough to know they weren't real. Although now, as he watched the woman hiding among the trees, he felt like he was in the middle of his very own scary movie. If he wanted to live, he had to be smarter than all the people who ended up dead in those movies. He couldn't make her angry, and he needed to keep her talking.

Cooper knew she'd grab him just as soon as he got close enough to her, so he took his time walking along the pond's edge. Once he stood in front of her, he turned his back so that he faced away from her. It took only a moment before the trees rustled behind him. He knew she would reach for him.

As her hands clasped around his mouth, he threw the rock into the water, allowing the stranger to take him away.

* * *

Her cottage had been a short ride away from the castle and, for the whole ride, Cooper sat with his eyes closed, praying that Morna would arrive soon. When nothing happened after she yanked him off the top of the horse and dragged him inside, Cooper knew he would have to keep her busy for a time—to keep her from harming him right away.

Cooper swallowed hard, hoping that his voice wouldn't shake as he talked. No matter how afraid he truly was, he didn't want his captor to know that. "Wow, this is some place you have here, lady. What's your name?"

To his surprise, she answered him with no hint of anger in her voice. For some reason, that frightened him more than it would have had she responded angrily. He realized she didn't want him scared because he would be more difficult to kill— like the time he'd joined Bebop on a deer hunting excursion— you couldn't scare the animals or they'd run.

"I'm Jinty. And what is yer name, lad?"

"Cooper."

Jinty nodded at him and pointed at a chair along the back wall.

Understanding, Cooper moved to sit as he grabbed onto the cup she extended in his direction. The smell was enough to make him pull up his nose in disgust. He knew in that instant that he couldn't drink whatever was inside.

"Drink up, lad. I know that I frightened ye. I dinna mean to. Me quarrel is no with ye. I doona wish to make it harder on ye than it needs to be."

He shook his head, handing it back to her. "No thank you,

ma'am. I'm not real thirsty."

She pushed it back in his direction. "I dinna ask ye if ye were thirsty."

Cooper held the cup cautiously, looking down at the thick brown liquid that smelled like the inside of his cousin Harry's diaper. How dumb did Jinty think he was? Had she never seen *Snow White?* The thought tickled him, and he accidentally laughed out loud for a brief moment. Of course she hadn't seen it—there were no movies here.

"I doona know why ye are laughing, lad, but ye best cease this instant. Now, drink."

Cooper knew he had to think of something fast. If he really drank it, he would die. He just needed to make her think he had, until Morna could get here.

"Do you have any sugar?" He asked hesitantly, worried she would get angry.

"Sugar? No, doona say another word to me until ye drink it, or I shall force it down yer throat."

Cooper swallowed hard, pushing away his fear. "I only wanted something to make it taste better so it will be easier to drink."

Jinty's eyebrows pulled together. "No a thing will make it sweeter, lad."

A sudden noise rapped against the window, and Cooper saw his opportunity. As Jinty jerked her head in the direction of the sound, Cooper quickly dripped some of the liquid onto the floor. Unfortunately, he didn't take into account that she would see the spill once she turned back in his direction.

All of Jinty's restrained anger released itself the instant she saw what he'd done, and he didn't have the chance to stand and run before she stood before him and gripped his face, forcing his mouth open as she poured the sticky liquid inside.

Cooper screamed and choked, but a flash of movement in the window behind Jinty caught his eyes. Within the next moment, the door to the cabin flew open to reveal Morna.

With the flick of Morna's wrists, the cup Jinty held against his mouth flew out of her hands and up against her face, crushing her nose as she fell to the ground unconscious.

Cooper sank from the chair as he ran toward Morna, throwing his arms around her legs. "I knew you would come, but I'm afraid you're too late. She made me drink it." Cooper sank down on the floor, suddenly feeling sleepy. He'd never expected to die this way—he'd always hoped he'd get to meet his end in a real-life *Jurassic Park*. "I'm guessing I'll die soon."

The laughter that erupted from Morna hurt his feelings. He always thought she liked him.

"Ach, lad. Do ye really think I'd let her kill ye? I saw her lifting the cup to yer lips, and I spelled it into prune juice. Other than a loose stool or two, I think ye shall survive."

Cooper exhaled a breath he hadn't known he held. "What? Are you telling me the truth?"

"Of course I am. Now, stand yerself up for we need to secure the beastly witch before she wakes up."

Cooper looked down at Jinty as he stood, wrinkling up his nose in disgust at the blood that was running down her face.

"What are you going to do with her?"

"Do ye want me to tell ye the truth, Cooper? Or do ye wish me to tell ye what I should tell a child?"

Cooper turned his head at her—of course she already knew his answer. "The truth…always."

"Aye, fine. I'll kill her lad. Once she wakes and we've had a bit of a discussion, I will put her in the ground. No one harms me family, lad. Does that bother you?"

Cooper didn't know what to think about that. It was wrong to kill people, but this woman had also meant to kill him. "Has she hurt other people?"

Morna nodded. "Many. She was nearly responsible for Eoghanan's death, and she would have killed ye too if ye hadna thrown the wee rock."

"E-o!" Cooper shook his head in disbelief. He liked E-o too much to imagine him dead. "Okay, do it, Morna. I don't want her to hurt anyone else. But..." he hesitated. He didn't wish for Morna to think him weak. "Don't hurt her. I don't think there's really any need for that."

Morna's face dropped in disappointment, but she nodded as she pointed outside the door of the cottage. "Aye, fine. Once she is awake, I willna cause her much pain, but now that she is asleep, I willna bring her around back carefully."

Cooper watched with wide eyes as Morna mumbled a spell underneath her breath and turned to leave the cottage. With each step, Jinty's body dragged along behind Morna on it's own, the blood from her nose leaving a nasty trail.

Chapter 44

The sight of Jeffrey collapsed next to a pool of his own blood and vomit brought me to my knees. Finding one of Cooper's shoes next to him sent me into hysterics. I could do nothing but scream and cry over Jeffrey's limp body as Eoghanan checked to see if he lived. His pulse was strong and steady which served as some small relief, though it did nothing to numb my panic over Cooper's absence.

It took only moments before my screams sent Baodan, Mitsy, and Charles running toward us from the castle. Within seconds of their taking in the scene, I was gathered up in Mitsy's arms as she tried to calm me.

"This poison is the same that was used on me the night of Osla's death, the same that our mother consumed for so long."

Eoghanan's voice was strong, but I could hear the panic and worry in it. The guilt he already felt at not disposing of the witch before now.

"'Tis Jinty, the witch that provided Niall the poison. I believe we passed her cottage on the way here."

"Aye." Baodan spoke next to him, reaching out to steady Charles who'd paled significantly. "Ye and Grace ride in the direction ye believe her to be at once, and I will send men after ye immediately. I will stay to aid in Jeffrey's recovery." He looked quickly to Charles and then to me. "He will recover. The poison in this dose is no meant to kill him."

I knew I would hyperventilate if I didn't get a grip on my panic. The over-rush of emotions would dull my senses, and I needed my wits about me in order to save Cooper. Grabbing onto Mitsy's hand, I pulled myself up and turned to re-mount our horse, saying nothing to Eoghanan who had already turned in the same direction.

He lifted me quickly onto the back of the horse, speaking

calmly to me as he mounted behind me. "She willna have hurt him, Grace. No yet. No without someone to witness it; without that, the act would be pointless, for none would know for certain if 'twas her. I promise ye, I will die before I let her hurt him or ye."

I breathed in deeply, boxing up any emotion that wouldn't serve to help me save my son. I'd be damned if I let that bitch hurt my son. She was a fool if she thought she would end the day any place other than six feet under.

A sharp groan from behind me caused me to turn my head, and I looked to see Mitsy leaning forward, one hand on her back.

She saw me staring and waved us onward, smiling through the pain. "Go on. Get out of here, the both of you. It's just…gas."

Eoghanan nodded and nudged the horse into a run, but not before I heard her scream once more in Baodan's direction.

"Holy shit, Baodan, my water broke."

* * *

I did nothing but pray for my son's safety as we galloped toward the pillar of smoke we'd seen earlier. It took us mere minutes to reach it, but it felt like days. I flung myself from the horse's back the instant Eoghanan pulled the beast to a stop, only pausing at the sound of Eoghanan's urgent voice behind me.

"Grace, no!"

His voice was as panicked and raspy as I'd ever heard it. Only when his arms came around me to refrain me from stepping toward the cottage did I see what he looked at.

A trail of thick, fresh blood ran down the steps of the cottage, marking a trail all the way to the back of it.

"No! Oh God, no!" Sobs racked my body as I collapsed in his arms, screaming uncontrollably.

"Grace." Eoghanan shook my shoulders roughly. "Grace,

shut yer mouth. This is no over, yet. The witch is still here. Now if ye canna stop yer screaming until we find her, I shall gag ye and strap ye to the horse."

The calmness of his voice shocked me into silence. How could he not be as lost in the thralls of grief as I was? I looked up into his eyes, ready to throttle him for not sharing my pain, when I understood.

His grief had been temporarily pushed aside by his rage. He would kill the witch for what she had done.

I said nothing, only choked back my tears for the second time and followed him around the cottage where he was forced to clamp his hands over my mouth once again to keep me from crying out in relief.

There, standing not fifty yards from us, was Cooper, his hands on both hips as he looked in the direction of the billowing smoke and the woman who stood in front of it—Morna.

It was only then, after my eyes adjusted to the shock of seeing Morna in such an unexpected place that my ears began to hear what she said to Jinty, who she had strapped up against a tree, panic in the young woman's eyes.

"If yer only transgression was being foolish enough to fall for Niall's lies, I suppose ye could be forgiven, but ye are responsible for the deaths of others. No only that, but ye tried to harm me family. No one does that, lass."

The witch Jinty snarled, thrashing against the magic chains which held her, as she spit in Morna's direction.

I threw a quick glance to Cooper who had yet to see us. I expected him to look afraid; instead, he looked fascinated. I wanted to run toward him but refrained, not wishing to interrupt the witch's confrontation.

"Ye can twist yerself about in these chains all day, curse me under yer breath all ye wish, but I am more powerful than ye will ever be, lass. Ye will die today, but take comfort that ye willna suffer. Ye can thank the boy for that. I will snap yer neck with the flick of me wrist before I toss ye into the flames."

"Do it." Jinty's words were raspy and hideous, the hatred in her eyes enough to chill me through. "But with me last breath, I damn ye and all yer…"

She was given no chance to finish her curse. Before her last words, there was a terrible crack, and the witch's head fell limp against her shoulder. The chains that held her body vanished, and she fell back into the flames, disappearing before all of our eyes.

Morna turned away from the flames and walked toward Cooper as we watched. She spoke to him gently. "Are ye alright, lad? I dinna mean to scare ye, but the lass was mad if she thought I'd let her curse me family at the end."

Cooper nodded, giving her a brief grin before his eyes finally shifted in our direction. As he ran toward me, Morna turned and addressed Eoghanan as if she'd known we'd been there all along.

"Eoghanan, for God's sake, release Grace. Jinty is gone now. Ye doona mean to keep her from hugging her son, do ye?"

"How are ye here, Morna?"

"Ach," Morna waved a dismissing hand toward the pillar of smoke. "Cooper sent for me."

Eoghanan released me, and I charged Cooper who wrapped his arms around me but pulled away as I clung to him. "What's the matter with you, Mom? Did you not have a good time on your honeymoon?"

"What? Cooper, are you joking? You were just kidnapped, and you think I'm upset because I didn't have a good time on my honeymoon?"

"But Mom…" he pulled back as far as he could in my vice-like hold on him. "I wasn't kidnapped. Not but for a minute, and I knew Morna was coming for me anyway so I just didn't worry too much."

"You didn't worry." The tone of my voice seemd to be frightening him more than anything else had so I struggled to pull it into one of some normalcy. "Cooper, you worry about everything."

"I didn't because of the red rock, Mom." He said it so plainly, as if I were the fool for not knowing what he meant.

Morna's spoke as she waved us all near to her. "Shall we return the three of ye to McMillan Castle? And Cooper," she reached out to pat his shoulder, "I think it might be best if ye allow me to explain."

Chapter 45

Whether it was really Cooper's red rock or just Morna's uncanny ability to know everything that went on with her family, no matter the century, no one cared. We all realized how unusual it was for her to make a travel herself—having not done so since she'd left her own time as a young girl.

She'd not only arrived in time to save Cooper, but to provide a remedy for Jeffrey, and to gift Mitsy with a, while not painless birth, certainly a more pleasant one. After the chaotic and emotionally draining afternoon, all was returned to right within the castle by evening.

Mitsy and Baodan welcomed their beautiful and ridiculously chunky baby boy, Rodric McMillan, at sundown. For the first time in his life, Cooper was out for the count before supper. His little adventure with the horrific witch, Jinty, had been far more traumatic on his parents and stepfather than it had been on him.

I sat on the edge of Cooper and Jeffrey's bed watching them both sleep when Eoghanan appeared in the doorway, his hand extended toward me.

"Come to bed, lass. I doona think either of them shall open an eye until morning."

I stood and, after kissing Cooper on the forehead, joined Eoghanan, taking his hand as we walked to our bedchamber. When we reached the doorway, I turned to stop him, gathering his face in my hands as I kissed him gently.

"My entire life, there have been only two men that I loved so much I couldn't measure it, couldn't get a grasp on how much they meant to me, couldn't fathom what my life would look like without them. Now…there are three. You are the person I didn't even know I wanted but needed so desperately. One day, I want to make two dozen more Coopers with you."

He ran his thumb along my brow, kissing me gently on the top of my head as he gathered me in his arms and carried me inside. "I want nothing more than that, Grace. But, lass, mayhap we doona start tonight."

I laughed as he lay me on top of the bed, nodding in agreement as we crawled beneath the covers in unison. For the first time in a week, we lay in each other's arms and slept like rocks.

It defined perfection.

Epilogue

Two Weeks Later

Cooper walked hand-in-hand with Morna to the pond's edge, his heart a little heavy at the thought of saying goodbye.

"Are you sure you have to leave? There's a bunch of rooms in this castle, and most of them are empty. Believe me, I know. I'm always sneaking inside them."

Morna squeezed his hand before bending to hug him. "Aye, Jerry needs me much more than all of ye. He canna cook to save his life. I worry he'll starve to death without me."

Cooper laughed, pulling one of the black stones out of his pocket and extending it in Morna's direction. "I guess you're right. Are you sure you want to go back this way? You get kinda wet."

"I think it only fair that I subject meself to the same treatment I did each of ye, aye?"

Cooper hugged Morna's neck before pulling away. "Yeah, I guess so, but I hope you're a good swimmer. Hey, can I ask you one more question before you leave?"

"Aye, what do ye wish to ask?"

"It's about my dad. He's so alone here. Everybody has someone else but him."

Cooper watched as Morna stood and smiled down at him, twirling the black stone through her fingers. "Ye are here for him."

He shook his head, exasperated. "I don't count. He needs somebody to kiss and stuff…like Mom and E-o."

Morna winked at him before she drew her arm back to let loose the stone, her words barely escaping her lips before the rock touched the water, and she vanished.

"All in due time, wee Cooper. All in due time."

Coming Summer 2014...

Jeffrey's story

IN DUE TIME—A NOVELLA

Book 4.5 of Morna's Legacy Series

Sign up for Bethany Claire's Newsletter to receive the most up-to-date information on this release.
http://bethanyclaire.com/contact.php#mailing-list

About the Author

Bethany Claire is the *USA TODAY* Bestselling Author of the Scottish Time Travel Romance novels in Morna's Legacy Series. They include *Love Beyond Time*, *Love Beyond Reason*, A Conall Christmas (A Novella), Love Beyond Hope, and her newest novel, *Love Beyond Measure*. She lives in the Texas Panhandle.

Connect with me online:

http://www.bethanyclaire.com

http://twitter.com/BClaireAuthor

http://facebook.com/bethanyclaire

http://www.pinterest.com/bclaireauthor

If you enjoyed reading *Love Beyond Hope*, I would appreciate it if you would help others enjoy this book, too.

Recommend it. Help other readers find this book by recommending it to friends, readers' groups and discussion boards.

Review it. Please tell other readers why you like this book by reviewing it at Amazon or Goodreads. If you do write a review, please send me an email to bclaire@bethanyclaire.com so I can thank you with a personal email. Or visit me at http://www.bethanyclaire.com

JOIN THE BETHANY CLAIRE NEWSLETTER!

Sign up for my newsletter to receive up-to-date information of books, new releases, events, and promotions.

http://bethanyclaire.com/contact.php#mailing-list

Acknowledgments

With every book, there are so many people that help along the way, and each of you have my eternal gratitude for your help in the process. I couldn't do it without any of you.

As always, thank you to Dee, for your suggestions and friendship.

To my proofreading team: Karen Corboy, Elizabeth Halliday, Marsha Orien, and Jan Powell, thank you for being another set of eyes and for your wonderful suggestions. I hope that you enjoyed the process as much as I did and that you'll be ready for the next book whenever I complete it.

To Damonza, for creating another fabulous cover. I think this is my favorite so far.

To both Rik Hall and Author E.M.S. for formatting—thank you for agreeing to work with me despite the super tight deadline.

Lastly, thank you to my Mom. You are really the backbone of my entire business and I couldn't do without your faith, patience, and encouragement. I am so excited for you to come to work for me. I promise not to work you too, too hard.

Books by Bethany Claire

Morna's Legacy Series

Love Beyond Time

Love Beyond Reason

Love Beyond Hope

A Conall Christmas — A Christmas Novella

Love Beyond Measure

In Due Time — A Novella

(Available Summer 2014)